They Called Him Faggot
A Novel

GQ Jackson

Thank you, JBJ. There are words that could describe what I feel for you. But, then they would, themselves, become a novel.

To Angel Jackson, Natalie Prudhomme, Barbara Spiller, Dalton Celestain, Sharhonda Watkins, Gabriel Watkins, John Augbon, Damon Thibodeaux, D. Wolverton, D. Riddick, K. Finger, A. Olivier, A. Guillory, K. Reynolds, A. Gray, R. Michael, R. Jefferson, D. Goodwin, A. Narcisse, and Clayton Washington.

A special thank you to Crystal Millner, D. Claiborne, Marvin Evans, James Doyle, Michelle Jenkins, Courtney Jones, Vaughndrea Siner, Lorena Caesar, and Geormario "Milan" Murray. Peace, love, and good vibes to all of you.

To Dr. Roshunda Belton for telling me I was a great writer every opportunity that she could and for kindly humbling me when I felt I was a great writer too early. I appreciate how much of a champion and big sister you have become to me. To Dr. Jennifer McMullen for gently forcing me to become an English major. To Dr. Mica Gould for hurting my feelings in her World Literature course when she told me one rainy morning that my writing is too flowery. I regret to report that this has not changed. Also, I want to thank Sherry Cato for being the kindest soul I have ever met in my life. I only hope to show your sympathy and empathy to whomever enters my life. I learned much from you during my time at Grambling State University in Grambling, Louisiana. To Dr. Michele Sabino for telling me that the best writing is rewriting. I dedicate this novel to you as I, ignorantly and stubbornly, allowed the first draft of it to become the final draft. Your encouraging words during the time in my master's program at the University of St. Thomas in Houston, Texas allowed me to find some morsel of a voice ensconced within myself. Finally, to Dr. Otiz "O.T." Porter for showing me how cool I will be as a professor soon. Thank you, specifically as the gay, black professor that seemed like a mirror's reflection, for showing me that being an asshole could actually work to my advantage.

And, to my siblings in college: Ebony Oliphant, Lawanda Sowell, and Jaderian Breshon Williams. Thank you for protecting me, taking care of me, and allowing me to be the nuisance that I was and still am. I will never forget the kindness all of you have shown me.

... [I despise social media]

I am Facebook friends with the man who raped me.
~~He's in medical school.~~
~~He has excelled academically, so there's a scholarship for high school students in his name.~~
~~He's a monster.~~
~~He's gorgeous, and I aspire to be as accomplished and successful as he is.~~
~~I don't know how to say that he raped me aloud.~~
~~Rape would imply that I am a victim.~~
~~And, I am not a victim.~~
~~I am a man.~~
~~A man who was raped at 1:16 AM on a Friday.~~
~~Are men raped?~~
~~Three women that I have randomly asked have told me no.~~
~~So, I am overreacting.~~
~~I continue to navigate my life without acknowledging that it ever occurred.~~
~~Is that normal?~~
~~I don't ever care to sit, reflect, and figure out the answer.~~
~~He's a successful black man;~~
~~educated;~~
~~ambitious;~~
~~philanthropic;~~
~~community-oriented;~~
~~unifying;~~
~~most of us are in jail—or, at least that's what they say in the media;~~
~~most of us are hoping to learn the lesson that success is tangible.~~
~~There are times in which I remember how kind he once was to me, how he was the most respectful man I had ever encountered in life.~~

~~He knows my story; I know his. We share a fraternal bond forged in attempting to climb out of the pool that is inherited generational darkness and aimlessness.~~
~~There is a scholarship in his name.~~
~~He allows kids to attend college with the money he donates and fundraises.~~
~~Those kids, our beautiful black kids, need that scholarship.~~
~~They deserve to go to college just as much as we did.~~
~~Red wine. That's what we were drinking.~~
~~I fucked up.~~
~~I drank too much.~~
~~I was weak.~~
~~I was careless.~~
~~I was too comfortable.~~
~~I didn't fight fiercely enough. In fact, I didn't fight at all after I realized his left palm covered my mouth. His right hand held my legs up. His weight held me down. I was drowning by the hands of someone who would soon swear his life to enriching the lives of others.~~
~~It's a theoretical abyss.~~
~~That's where you go mentally when you are raped.~~
~~You leave your body there with them, ignoring what they are doing so you can safely travel to that safer place.~~
~~What the fuck happened?~~
~~I am reminded again that vulgarity in writing cheapens your work, my former professor's voice in my head.~~
~~This is what I am talking about.~~
~~I think about what others feel even in a moment in which I should be the only voice.~~
~~Is God tired of hearing the noise that comes from everyone's goddamn mouths all the time?~~
~~I've never said or written goddamn in my entire life. I think white people are rubbing off on me.~~
~~I think I am trying to be normal.~~
~~I think I am strong.~~

~~I think I can handle everything that life throws my way.~~
~~I think that because he is black and successful and fortuitous and determined, I think it is a horrible idea to mess that up for him.~~
~~I think…I'm tired of thinking.~~
~~I say his name aloud when I am alone in the shower, all of the rancor in my voice having dissipated over these three years.~~
It's hard.

the gayest presuppositions

I heard him say, the color of the sun. Your skin is the color of the sun. Every single human being. Warmth is what you should give to the world.

That's what the t-e-l-e-v -a-n-g-e-l-i-s-t—I pretentiously declare each letter aloud to the universe—says on channel 7 or 8. I can't remember which of the 8 channels he's on.

We don't have electricity often enough to memorize channels and the times of shows.

I sit on the ash gray couch from the Salvation Army with my feet tucked underneath my legs and peer out of our damaged white blinds, the handiwork of a five-year-old who must be in the know about every single occurrence that happens outside of this grumpy, off-white two-bedroom house. All six of us live here. I am aware of this and am awake being a parent because thinking about the future of the family is what parents do.

It is 3:42 AM, and I notice the sky is a gentle, sleepy purple that exists so far beyond the broken blinds that are so characteristic of ~~homes~~ houses in the 'hood. The hood is not home to me. It is home to poverty and a single mother taking care of five kids by three fathers. I've heard other women viciously discuss my mother and her supposed inability to keep her legs closed. I am ashamed to be the product of her losing her virginity. I feel disgusting as if it were me who defiled her the moment I began developing in her belly. She is poor because of me, because of my brothers and sisters and me. This is what I think about during the commercials—when I'm not listening intently to a white man speak about the Jesus who looks like him.

He comes back on and begins talking about the current blessings in our [each and every individual viewer's] lives.

Current blessings?

I look about the living room and imagine that I can see the heat. This is why I am the darkest one in my family, I wish to say to him. It's because this goddamned heat bakes me alive. I'm a fortune cookie left in the oven (is that even how they are made?), my intelligence comparable to the slip of paper someone would recognize as my fortune denigrated by oven-like temperatures (I guess I have decided that this is, indeed, how they are made).

But, I say none of that since the t-e-l-e-v-a-n-g-e-l-i-s-t is still speaking and advises us to think about the beautiful future that God has already created for us and is patiently waiting for us to experience.

Next month, I'll be thirteen-years-old, and closer to dying and leaving behind four children who count on me to cook and clean and be a parent since my mother is always at work. Next month we'll be sleeping with the windows open again, the mosquitoes feasting on our bodies as we lie on blankets that scratch like metallic nails in heat that even my imagination couldn't have conjured up. That isn't a fucking blessing. That isn't the work of Jesus Christ. That isn't the work of God.

I want to tell the t-e-l-e-v-a-n-g-e-l-i-s-t that on those summer nights I am charred alive and this is actually why my skin is the color of the sun, but I hold my tongue so that I don't rudely interrupt his sermon (that's what I've heard my grandmother call them—these speeches that people speaking for God deliver). But the t-e-l-e-v-a-n-g-e-l-i-s-t is kind and warm. He tells me that I matter, that God created me for a specific purpose that is amazing and great and impacts the world.

But, in my experience, black boys do not agree with the t-e-l-e-v-a-n-g-e-l-i-s-t. They would say he is lying, say I am lame, say I am stupid, say I am a faggot, say God doesn't love me, say that the t-e-l-e-v-a-n-g-e-l-i-s-t shouldn't love me.

This one particular black boy, my neighbor, is not like the t-e-l-e-v-a-n-g-e-l-i-s-t; he is cruel and is the color of a fortune cookie definitely left too long in the oven (even longer than me, if I were a fortune cookie) and doesn't have blue eyes. He calls me a nigga and says I'm just like the rest of them. He says we are the same.

This is not what the t-e-l-e-v-a-n-g-e-l-i-s-t said at 10:34

PM the night before, his words affirming me and reminding me that I am a special snowflake for God that is unique and made for a special purpose.

No one in my family ever graduated high school, so I don't know if they even know what a purpose is, but I want to know what mine is. Four more years and I'll graduate. I tell myself that is the first step to finding purpose.

The neighbor boy slashes at me with a sharpened pencil from his backpack. I dodge his sword. He pushes me with all of his force and I feel myself floating as I hit the wet ground, the breath evacuating from my lungs with urgency as if he's intimidated them as well. Grass stains are graffiti upon my khaki pants. He is on top of me and his fists feel like thunder striking my face. No one helps me. I learn that we watch people hurt until we hurt, and only then is it that we encounter a moment in which we suddenly care. I'll have to scrub these pants all night in the tub before my mama catches me wearing them, begging to be an embarrassment to her. She doesn't like feeling as though we are a charity case.

Only the white people from the Pentecostal church five minutes away are allowed to know about us not having any money or food. They bring us a frozen turkey and thousands of boxes of macaroni for Thanksgiving.

But, no one in the 'hood can know that we have nothing. Angel has made sure that we know (well, at least the first four of the five of us as Azhia recently asked a white woman for ten dollars in Wal-Mart and was pretty damn proud of herself for doing it) better than to do that.

This boy calls me a poor nigga (he actually says po' nigga) and walks away.

But, I've been taught to say poor, door, and four correctly. I feel sorry for him, mostly because he probably doesn't have a mother who learned how to be white. I know what he means, though. I understand black.

He's right—my neighbor.

The t-e-l-e-v-a-n-g-e-l-i-s-t, a white man on TV with a

perfect white smile and a gorgeous blue tailored suit (I'll never own one of those) now seems insidious to me. He lied right to my face when he told me I was special. I almost believed that he had seen my face as he peered into the camera while his voice permeated the living room I was lying in, listening to him, holding on to his every word because there is nothing else except an invisible hope of escape to hold on to in the 'hood.

    I'm a poor nigga.

    Does this white man know what that entails?

    Poor people don't have purpose. I suppose that is why they are poor in the first place.

    Niggas, especially, don't have purpose.

the house that I remember

at 4211 Worthy Drive
when the city turns the water off
we cannot shower
but we do cry.
because of these tears
we still have water even when
my drunken stepfather drinks up all the money
we made this month selling food stamps
to our neighbors.

Tea, with lemon

Wine is what we drink four glasses of.
Red wine. Cheap. They were about $13 a bottle, so I had purchased two of them two weeks prior to his visit.

I remember the wine merchant, a friendly white man who'd shown me more respect and acknowledgement that anyone in Arkansas at that point. He'd suggested it. Perhaps he was being nice because I was spending money. But I would like to think that $30 or so every two weeks wasn't enough to pretend to be happy to see me, to have conversation with me, to even sometimes offer me a discount.
His name isn't memorable, but I remember his face. There are people like this in the world—people who have shown you kindness that you'll remember for the rest of your existence. Yet, somehow in the spatial layout of life, your trajectory in life doesn't allow you to ever bump into them again.
I left the liquor store excited to be seeing my friend a couple of hours later. It was right after I had left school—my students were especially cooperative that day. Tenth-graders—virtually all of them—on their best behavior the entire day was strange.

It never struck me that he planned on spending the night, even though he first knocked on my door shortly after 9:30 PM.
We spent most of the time before midnight in the living room, its shabby tan carpet comforting as we rolled around and howled in laughter at all things life. He was hilarious, warm, and intelligent, and this is why I trusted him wholly. A funny man—one whose view on life seemed not-too-serious-like-mine—was what I needed in those lonely moments in Arkansas. Another black body who could understand who I was and what I was trying to find in life as a lost twenty-two-year-old.

It is pitch black—darker than his lovely skin—and I cannot see anything in my bedroom, my space in this universe, but I see all of him, mentally. As he thrusts, I feel more drunk, more intoxicated, more inebriated, pathetic even. I am a feeble fish caught by a fisherman who fails to see his cruelty in gaining happiness through my suffering, his hook stabs me over and over and over and over again and I lie there knowing that it will hurt more if I move. His body is on top of mine and my legs are pushed against my chest and there is nowhere to run. I bite my raised right arm to stop myself from making any sound. I refuse to motivate him with a groan, moan, or sigh. I stop breathing. It hurts more to fight it. When I can no longer hold my breath, I allow my lungs to take in air and then let it out slowly.

Again, I am touching the universe—a blackness that is indescribable—his skin is almost as dark as shadows dancing on waves of a pool at midnight. It is then that I recall the events that have led to this moment, a penetration un-avoided. His arms wrap around my body in a platonic hug that causes me to laugh. He's always been goofy. And handsome. He's been an amazing friend to me when I've needed advice and emotional support. He has been the black friend that I think does our people justice. He is a good person, I once thought.

I remember him smiling only a few moments before he turned the lights off.

His strokes are like a clock's ticks, rhythmic and depressing. I've never wanted to be older, but in this moment I wish to be old and free and unbothered by the monsters that exist on this earth. He keeps going, ignoring me and treating my body with the same reverence a child who has received his first magnifying glass would offer ants who crawl upon the ground. He destroys my temple, pouring gasoline onto my ant pile and unapologetically dropping a match on it. This half-sturdy temple is not ready for this. I am already lost in the tunnels of my mind. I cannot remember how to build one's self after your infrastructure has been fucked out of you—the kindness drained as if a pond could never thrive in your presence. Trauma invites mental acuity. Ants can rebuild; I cannot.

    I think of my boyfriend and of how he is peacefully asleep in another state, probably dreaming of me.
    We are drinking green tea in his dreams. He knows how much I love tea with honey. Tea is a liquid that exposes the beauty of life through taste. I breathe in its scent, happy and energetic.
    I am twenty-three years old; I don't deserve to be the victim. I should fight and scream and kick and spit and bite. I don't. I lie still, forced into my position of a folded doll under the control of a ventriloquist who was never this dark, never this cruel, never this disrespectful.
    Blackness hides my hand when I hold it up and reach for the ceiling. I see nothing, yet I feel like I am rising, and I can touch the ceiling fan that will spin me round and round so that I become sick and vomit. All of it will pour out of me. Then, I'll be clean. I'll feel free, I'll feel normal again. I reach out for God. I think she/he/it hears me and I feel light. I can fly.
    He grunts and sweats. He doesn't say thank you, he doesn't check on me, he doesn't allow me to move, he doesn't wipe the tears that streak across my face like runaway children that I encourage with my bout of silence, he doesn't comfort me, he only fucks me.
    When it is over six minutes later, I take a shower. It is fifteen after one in the morning. My drunkenness is gone, and I want it back—I long to feel numb and vulnerable so that I can become invulnerable and giddy enough to laugh at jokes and the hilarious things in life. A two-hour shower isn't long enough to cleanse me of the guilt that I feel. I am not absolved and the water that smells faintly of lead is not holy. I think about the phone calls and the text messages and our friendship and how I should not have said yes when he asked to come over while he was passing through the city I live in. I think about how I

allowed him to enter my safe space with a Trojan horse, filled with recreations of himself. I think that I am stupid. I think that crying is a sign of weakness, especially because I didn't do anything to hurt him like he hurt me. I think of rushing into my bedroom where he is sleeping in my bed and stabbing him, just as he has stabbed me over and over and over again.

    My shower ends. I slowly walk into my room and lie in bed. He is asleep yet seems to instinctively move closer to me to place his arm over my body. I lie with my eyes open for the next four and a half hours until it is time for me to leave my bedroom—my space that has been invaded and conquered and vandalized—for work. He kisses my cheek and I say nothing. He holds me for several seconds, in an attempt to offer me a hug that attempts to convey that offers me compassion and solace. I do nothing.

    Have a great day, he says.

    I look into his eyes, disappointed in myself.

    Have a great day, I robotically reply.

    He leaves and returns to Tennessee.

    I drive on the narrow streets of El Dorado, Arkansas for a little before reaching my destination.

    My high school students and I analyze the poetry of Gwendolyn Brooks that day.

    My rapist is a nurse. Not a monster in the eyes of society, but someone who helps and saves every single day. He is the hero in ocean blue scrubs and white non-slip shoes.

questioning myself in the shower

who will love me when my mother dies?

Black gay men don't need a therapist; we need a shot of cognac in a dimly-lit gay bar

Where is she when my uncle is sticking his erect penis into my mouth and forcing me to virtually swallow the entire thing? I choke and gag, and this seems to excite him. God probably had to turn her head away—I wouldn't have been able to stomach the sight of that either.

To be twenty-five-years-old is to be nine-years-old again, to be utterly vulnerable to the will of another who is older and succumbing to the burden of being a teenager.

After he ejaculates into my mouth, I am forgotten wrapping paper on Christmas at a suburban home. I am disposed of, relieved from my post, tarnished, and ascribed hand-me-down adjectives.

There is a saltiness that lingers on my tongue even sixteen years later. I don't talk about it, though.

Black families don't talk about shit like this.

How do you begin a conversation so intimate with people who don't even want to acknowledge that they don't truly know one another, know what each other are capable of, know what each other has done that has affected the lives of any of the others?

I'm a man, and I have been taught that men don't wallow on in the hopes of becoming a victim—this is what my father has wished I could learn and prove my proficiency of.

twenty-six

To be twenty-six-years-old is to be a newborn. I recognize nothing about myself.

Even after four years, the taste of my lover's lips is a taste best described as indescribable. No other adjective suffices.

Depression feels like lying in the sun nude and vulnerable, and unaware that perpetual confrontation with sunshine means vehemently chafed skin.

I remember lying in the sun as a child and falling asleep underneath a star that had warmed the air around me to ninety-four degrees on that day. I awoke, my body burning so badly that even my conscience felt like it had been stunned and stupefied. There was nothing my Aunt Charity could do, so her ex-husband gave me ointment that did not work at all in easing my pain. I later discovered that what he had given me was used for jock itch. My lips were left in a swollen, itching state. There was nothing we could do for the pain except place ice upon my lips and wait patiently for the swelling to recede. That pain taught me a valuable lesson that pretty things are dangerous when not enjoyed in moderation.

Why is pain necessary for growth?

I asked myself that one day as I stood in the rain, waiting for a sign from God. From an individual named Jesus Christ. From some fucking one.

While everyone at my grandmother's house ate inside for some gathering of family, I decided that I needed an escape—an intervention. Being alone was always a gift I was thankful for. Being in a two bedroom house with five other beings was draining enough.

I had stolen a cigarette from my stepfather, stashed it in my right pocket and carried it all the way to 1508 S. Walton St.

I stood outside and held the strange item in my hand,

careful not to crush it as I did view it as some life force that people drew some type of strength from. Why else would they stand outside in rain, in the cold sleet, in the rare and wet Louisiana snow to taste it—to feel the nicotine rush through over ? Why else would they decide that it was important enough to smell of it, to have its odoriferous nature imbued in the fibers of clothing and their pores?

    I gagged at the taste.

After preparing for an interview for 3 entire weeks;

      Being forced to drink a gallon of bad coffee. Horrible coffee, actually. And then having to vomit for the entire day. That's what receiving an email that says,

> Hi Gaquez,
> I hope you are doing well. We have finally completed our interview process, and we all agreed that you were an incredibly strong candidate for the position, one of our top three choices. At this time, however, we have extended an offer to one of the other candidates and they have accepted. We would love to keep your resume on file should another position become available.
>
> Lindsey, Elizabeth, Cathy, and I really enjoyed getting to know you better and feel like you would be an incredible asset to any education program. We wish you well and hope you will keep in touch with us.
>
> Sincerely,
> Amanda

feels like.

introspection introspection introspection introspection introspection introspection

 cascades of sweat along my spine
 and forceful thrusts are what I remember
 from my first time even though he promised
 to be gentle with my body
 and now I regret not asking him
 why do men
 crave god
 only to defile it
 as it lies before them
 on a twin bed in a freshman dormitory

Artist

      a man I once knew—he taught me how to
      smoke weed
      while he cooked spaghetti
      and burnt French bread that crunched but softened upon
my tongue—
         talked about his
         life experiences
         and then we made love twice.
         he was an artist;
         Artist.
         but artists never call back.
         that,
         in itself,
         is an artform.

you are becoming a man, boy. you need to get a haircut. and, years later...

The barbershop smells of oppression. [I am reminded, at 12:35 PM, that [in their eyes and even my own] I am not a man].

my brother stopped respecting me when they called me faggot

my uncles,
men
who eat gumbo in winter and summer,
call us outside in the heat of the day
in Louisiana where men sweat to show they are strong
and ask us to punch the side of my grandmother's house
that is made of red, sunburnt brick
where the scales of fish sliced and gutted,
by the coarse, fat hands of my grandfather
who is an embodiment of the black man in every single aspect
of its beauty,
ricocheted leaving dried white and gray scars
upon orange that is indescribable and yet
remains my favorite color,
but my uncles
called us outside and told me to punch the brick
why—I ask
show you are a man—they say
do it, nigga—they say

my uncles,
men
who beat their women and make love after,
call us outside in the heat of the day
in Louisiana where men fight to show they are brave
and ask us to punch the side of my grandmother's house
that is made of brick
red as flames
spilled oil has created on her stove,
that she elegantly, skillfully, innovatively
utilizes in the creation of gourmet meals
from food that poor people can afford,
but created, nonetheless,
by the hands of a stocky, tall woman
who is an embodiment of the black woman in
every single aspect of its beauty,
whose house we stand outside of
when my uncles
called us outside and told him to punch the

punch that shit—they say
and I hesitate
because where is the logic in
punching brick
stop being pussy, nigga—they say
Jackson niggas ain't soft—they say
earn this fucking last name—they say
then I don't want to be a Jackson—I say
and they stop loving me,
turning their backs on me
becoming hardened as a brick wall I am supposed to strike—
they called me faggot
this means to be inquisitive is to be feminine.

brick
ok—my brother says without hesitating
that's a fucking man—they say
yeah, nigga—they say
punch that shit—they say
fuck that blood, you're a man—they say
you ain't pussy, nigga—they say
Jackson niggas ain't soft—they say
you earned this fucking last name—they say
I'm a Jackson—he says
and they love him,
their bond strengthened and hardened as a brick wall my younger brother strikes—
they called him nigga
this means to be obedient is to be masculine.

he taught me that you can use water instead of milk

I bake cornbread
that tastes like cake.
I am learning how
to create things
that taste
sweeter than you.

strong woman in Louisiana

my grandmother has had   four   husbands
lost   four   husbands
and I wonder
how she picked up the million pieces after the first
how she picked up thousands of pieces after the second
how she picked up the twenty or so pieces after the third
how she picked up the two or three shards after the fourth
when I've cut myself attempting to lift myself
to even look down at the broken heart before me.
it feels so much better sitting indian-style
on the floor where there is no risk of falling
because your knees are already pressed against linoleum.

katrina twelve years later

does one grasp how the only people to cry out after a
hurricane are the survivors. you might as well have
stabbed me and let me bleed out. gotten it over with.
you're a monster for sparing my life even as I neared
death that has to be better than the void I feel now. you
deserve to sit in prison until you love me again.
bananas don't last in this apartment.
you are allergic to them
and I keep their taste
upon my lips
so as to keep you away.

a book of lavish proportions

In one of the Lake Charles public libraries that I frequented for its free internet access, I had read from an article on some illuminating site online that becoming gay was a process—that it was "*a fabulous time, sweetheart.*"

And, I clung to that printed article as if it were my Louisiana Bible, one rewritten specifically for a sixteen-year-old like me; young, lost, desperate, excited. Its words beckoned me, chided me, ridiculed me for stalling. I was taking my time and I knew it. I was afraid. Afraid of the fabulous time and how it would change my life, how it would somehow add an unnecessary amount of silver and an annoying shade of purple glitter to every aspect of my existence.

My heart beat frantically as I printed it out, nervous that the librarian would catch me and tell everyone. I almost suffered a heart attack—being fabulous was horrifying.

That article became my bible of lavish proportions. I read it every morning and night word for word in some hope of allowing its fabulousness to penetrate my soul.

I carried its folded and abused pages with me even as I went to work at McDonald's.

McDonald's had been offering me more hours and I avariciously accepted them. I awoke and went to school. I left school and went to work. I awoke and skipped school. I went to work.

Independence was what I wanted. Becoming officially gay is what I craved. Protected in my pocket, the article became a source of peer pressure. Gays needed money, or at least that's what I had read. We lived these lavish lifestyles, always surrounded by friends and mimosas and art that we had bought from our friends who, of course, were gay artists.

I was sixteen, single, closeted, and broke. Though, the article taught me to never admit such things. Being gay was an art form. Self-confidence was everything. And, you couldn't be confident by focusing on what you weren't. "*You have to use what you have, honey.*"

I had not become gay, yet—having a man say he was *your* man was required for one to actually become gay. I needed a man, and I didn't know how to get one. Wal-Mart wasn't exactly selling, and the irrevocably young and perverse Craigslist wasn't on my radar, or anyone's for that matter, in the retirement mecca of Louisiana.

On a school night, I met him while I was at work. I had seen him there a couple of time before, always reading a book or the newspaper at eight or nine at night. It was peculiar and fascinating at the same time.

That night he was wearing a red T-shirt and worn denim jeans that weren't impressively gay. His white athletic shoes were dirty, and his black belt matched with nothing he wore. He was vaguely attractive yet seemed impossible to talk to. I walked up to him—unafraid of rejection, mostly because I would pretend to just ask him questions out of boredom.

He said he was thirty-four. *But, he has wrinkles.* He said he worked for the news station. *Have I seen him on TV? I don't think so. But, we don't have cable, so I won't embarrass myself by asking questions that could scare him away.* He said he drove a BMW. *I only see a Honda Accord and a slightly battered navy-blue truck in the parking lot. Maybe he walked here to grab a bite to eat.* He told me I was handsome. *I am? Of course, I am. Gays have to be handsome in order to qualify as being really gay. He's telling me the truth. Would he lie?* He said he could pick me up during the weekend to take me to the mall and buy me anything I wanted. *Anything? I am becoming gay! This is the life!*

* * *

My mother couldn't know. I was her surrogate spouse and my siblings' caretaker, and I needed a break.

I am going to a friend's house. He and his dad are coming to pick me up. You haven't met this friend. His name is John, I told her.

Her questioning was fairly easy to maneuver.

Still, I could feel her brown eyes watching me through the window's blinds as I left the house at 9 PM that night to walk down the street to a navy-blue truck.

My body shook with nervousness and excitement as he mostly drove, and I mostly talked about high school problems that I faced as a teenager. He listened to it in stride and even offered advice as to what I should do in my attempts to remain in the closet and out of people's gossip circles.

His nervousness was revealed in him welcoming me into his place. He stumbled over his words when offering me water, and he chuckled a few times while giving me a short tour. His apartment was modest, and hardly capable of being described as lavish. I refused to allow him to destroy my opportunity to be gay. I imagined the writer of the article dismissing us both for not being gay enough.

We sat down on his coal black loveseat, and I noticed that it was littered with white, long hair. The snow-white cat appeared from nowhere, and I cringed. Cats weren't gay-friendly.

He pulled out a cigarette, presumably to calm his nerves, and lit it with a candle that was burning and resting on the coffee table. Cigarettes weren't gay-friendly.

His living space lacked a sense of direction and couth— I'd read an online post about how great the gays were and their special abilities.

Our dialogue seemed copied and pasted from a theatrical failure. I found myself inspecting the apartment and its walls for signs of his job, his family, his life. *Where is the BMW?* I realized I had to get out of there. He had lied to me. He was definitely not living the gay, lavish lifestyle that I wanted for myself. He began to talk about his news career.

I do a lot writing for the people you see on TV, he said. Cynthia Arceneaux? You see her on the news every single day. You've seen her, right? I see her all the time around this neighborhood. I think she lives a few streets down. She is actually—

Take me home, I interrupted him.

I succinctly explained myself as he drove me home, silently: I don't think I like men, I said.

I lied to him, and I liked it.

I exited the navy-blue truck and didn't care to say goodbye. He drove off and took his cheapness with him at 10 PM.

I exhaled before entering our home, wishing I could tell my mother everything. But, the mystique in knowing that I had spent time with an unknown man made me feel gayer and more lavish than I'd ever felt in my life. I chose to keep it all to myself.

Why'd you come back, she asked.

They had a cat, and everything smelled like cigarettes, I replied.

Why are people so disgusting and cheap, she responded as her face became contorted in disgust. There was something comforting in a poor woman criticizing others for *living* poor— that was much different from being poor.

I wondered if my mother was gay.

bending me upon repair

With no reference for how pliable my body is
I discovered
you did me a favor
breaking me in half;
it was precisely in that moment
that I found all of my warmth
hiding in the depths of a body cold to the touch
all of it spilling out like the change
of a ceramic piggy bank
owned by a white seven-year-old girl
who had not one care in the world
but to shatter what held her treasure
so that she could bathe in its brilliance.

and what was once free cost me $40

    someone told me something that only you knew—
    you were my therapist before my therapist
    and the injustice lies in the fact that you did not sign a confidentiality contract
    and that you can tell anyone that my naked body is littered with spots of discoloration
    and that I curse wildly during orgasm
    and that I like the scent of your neck
    and that…

Dalton

he rides in the sun for hours.
my grandfather cuts
the green grass
often
because he would have been lynched
for cutting any of the white people
who scared him mercilessly
in his childhood.

growth

I've come in from running in the rain
water cleansing me with its fingertips
baptizing a black gay man in non-denominational glory.
I felt one with God.
I felt one with myself.
Why is that one can lose touch with himself,
that losing himself becomes so easy?
And, more important than feeling one with myself?
The fact that I   F E L T.

knowing at the age of six

Before I even knew the concept of love and Valentine's Day and all of the hoopla concerned with pink and red, I gave a washed-to-many-times stuffed bear my mother had gotten from Goodwill to a classmate. Honestly, I had stolen the bear since it was actually intended for one of her boyfriends at the time. I figured he didn't need it. Grown-ups were rich. Or, so I thought when I was a child. My first-grade teacher, in her pleasant Oklahoman drawl, had explained, "You give something nice and pretty to the person that you love."

I figured I loved D'Marea Brown, so I gave that horrible-looking brown teddy bear to him. I was beyond proud of myself and beamed at it in all of its glory when I presented it to him. He took it from me and replied with an unbiased, "Thank you." Our classmates looked at us with indifference and we continued to build block structures and secretly play with glue that we allowed to dry upon the shallow crevices and fissures of our not-yet-worn hands.

That was when love was accepted. That was when love was genuine.

These thoughts cross my mind in the moments following the sound of his zipper. I bite into the pillow to ease the pain of his ungentle thrusts. Rough hands grasp my waist and force is applied to the small of my back. His breathing becomes more labored as the discomfort I feel becomes exponentially intensified. I assume that this is what it means to feel love. This is what it feels to have someone want you. To have someone want to be inside of you. To have sex with one of the senior frat boys. To be in college for only a few months and already have a man deeply in love with you. Beads of sweat fall off of his forehead and drip drop drip upon my shoulders. I don't mind since they provide me an opportunity to forget the excruciating feeling of his penis being shoved inside of me. I never hear his voice during the entire ten minutes. There is no moment of

romantic dialogue or a check to see if I am alright. No kiss upon my lips to remind me of why I am doing this. There is a reluctance to gaze into my eyes, even when I turn the upper half of my body to look at him. Refusal to acknowledge me and the beauty he apparently saw in me during his pursuit of me and leading up to the moment of penetration.
    This is what it means to have sex.
    With a man.
    For the first time.

before I left for Havana, Cuba

I kissed you for the first time
at 1116 Jackson Blvd
and there was an immediate regret
in knowing
that I was sharing valuable morsels of myself
opening up a heavy wooden door to allow you in
and nothing would be left
once you tasted me.

your mother ~~and father~~ raised a fool

I have lived in Houston for three years
and I am still lost on every highway
but I know three ways
to get to your house.
what would your mother and father say
if I walked in and drank
water from the glasses in the left cabinet that we are
allowed to use?
they'd wonder how I know their home so well
but you'd never tell them how many hours of my life
I spent in love with you
in that place.

feeling

my therapist says that eventually I have to feel something but, I want to feel *you* inside of me.

habits

Things I once did happily before meeting you:

- Danced in the shower
- Cooked with passion
- Painted utterly awful masterpieces upon white canvases
- Looked forward to the transformations of the moon
- Allowed the ocean to touch me, baptize me, cleanse me
- Cried when a beloved character in a movie died
- Cried when a beloved character in a movie realized they had fallen in love
- Wrote poetry
- Rode a bike and allowed the wind's fingers to slash at my face
- Appreciated the beauty of colors, even gray and white and tan
- Sang while washing dishes
- Prayed
- Read the dictionary and learned a new word every single day
- Ate dried apples
- Marveled at the vivid colors of bananas
- Daydreamed
- Liked the scent of gasoline

Now I:
- Shower quickly
- Cook without all of the shenanigans of a foolish chef

- Complain about the price of paint and canvases
- Keep up with the moon's cycle using the app on my Apple watch
- Realize the ocean is a dirty place
- Have no sympathy of characters who die in movies
- Scoff at how stupid a character who has fallen in love appears
- Focus on technical writing employed in emails that seem much more important than the frivolities of poetry
- Would rather run than ride a bike since I no longer trust anything or anyone to carry me forward except myself
- Don't see or appreciate colors
- Neglect the trivial practice of prayer
- Rush throughout my day utilizing the least amount of brain power possible
- Eat fruit for the nutrients and nothing else
- Concentrate on what is important in life—harsh reality that life is hard
- Go as far as possible on an almost empty tank so that I don't have time to think because thinking means thinking of you

Dalton and us

don't, *my grandfather says in his almost-baritone voice,* ever look a white person in the eyes, don't be threatening, stop being loud, you'll draw attention to yourself, try to blend in, don't speak unless it's absolutely necessary, be kind, I don't care if they aren't kind to you, be kind to them, that's how the world works, don't be hard-headed, you'll understand all of this when you're older and looking for a job, listen to your grandmother, yes I know she makes you go to church, it's for your own good, oh you don't believe in God, be quiet and don't ever tell her that, don't be hard-headed, listen to your mama, yes I know she's young and that she makes mistakes, you'll know how to be a better parent, graduate from college and be better, oh, that's right, you are graduating next month, time flies, you are growing up, how is college, what do you mean you're depressed and ready to quit, don't be afraid of anyone, not even the future, look people in the eyes, be assertive, but don't be too black, be yourself, don't be loud, don't be threatening, I tell you that all the time, be better, speak up, be respectful, yeah I stopped going to church for the same reason, no matter if we are not together she still means the world to me, your grandmother is still your grandmother even if I'm not there, don't be hard-headed, use white people to get what you want, but they'll only like you if you're nice, oh you thought we didn't know about you, it's ok, you're still my grandson, I can't see the way I used to, my vision is slowly slipping away, I'm getting surgery soon, could one of you boys cut the grass, they're trying to take my driver's license from me, these glasses hurt my head, your brother stole $500 from me, yeah he wrote a check to himself and deposited it into his bank account, I know, I know, it really hurt my feelings that my own grandson could do that, no don't apologize for him, well your baby brother is dating a white girl, I told him to be careful about her family, I don't trust it one bit, happy father's day to you too, you're a father to your sisters and brothers, thank you, yeah I know today is my birthday, yeah I know your birthday is tomorrow, tell your grandmother I said hello when you go to visit her in a few, cut her grass while you're there, I'm sad it didn't work out, that's life, we both really tried for this second time, they're trying to get me to retire, they don't like that I'm the only black man telling a bunch of white men what to do, I have to get my eyes checked soon, they are watching me at work, your brother was in jail too, I didn't know that you didn't know, it was going to take $1800 to get him out, they dropped the charges, he got out last night, I don't know where he stays, when you get the time call me, yeah I saw that video of a black man being shot, was he unarmed, well that happened all the time when I was growing up, they are not going to stop until they get a racial war started, I miss you too, I love you, yeah I know I never say that, oh you're writing a poem for me, read it to me soon.

thank the lord; (a nod to me not being to church more than twice in almost ten years)

My grandmother whispers, Thank the Lord. . .*she says,* get up, it's Sunday, don't talk too loudly while my gospel music is on, wash your face, come eat this waffle and scrambled eggs, I don't care if you don't like eggs, drink your water, didn't I say I don't care if you like something or not, do what I say, brush your hair, let me brush your hair because obviously you don't know how to do it, don't tell me it hurts because you don't know nothing 'bout pain, hurry up and get dressed, take off those blue socks and put on the black ones, you need to match, are these underwear clean, you better pee before we leave, what you mean you don't have to pee, go make yourself pee, well don't ask me later, hurry up and get in this car, we will only listen to gospel music in my car so don't ask to play that rap music, I don't want to hear nothing 'bout Aaliyah, I don't care what she sings, It's all rap to me, hurry up and get in this church, we're late, don't you dare go up to the front, let's sit somewhere at the back, no you cannot go to the bathroom, sit up straight, close your mouth before a fly gets in, tuck in that shirt boy, stop looking around when someone is leading prayer, when we are praying keep your eyes closed, open your eyes now because we are done praying, stand up for this musical selection, sit down, the pastor is about to speak, pay attention, no not to me but to the pastor, be quiet, stop inspecting your fingers and inspect the Word, come closer to me so I can swat you for disrespecting God, no you cannot go to the bathroom, you're going to understand all of this when you're older, you better listen to what our pastor is saying, don't make me slap you for saying he isn't your pastor, wake up, do you want God to punish you for falling asleep during the Word, hurry up before there's a line to get out of here, Thank the Lord we made it home, you hungry, go take off your church clothes and get in some regular clothes, go outside and play, I'll call you in when the food is ready, love you, too.

black *feels* like

the color that your skins *feels* is black sunshine that simultaneously tinges your skin with a permanent stain and liberates it; it is happy, it is the way your grandmother smiles at you, it is the way your brother bullies you but fights anyone else who bullies you, it is the way your mother tells you she loves you, it is the way your mother whips you with a belt and then tells you that she loves you, it is the way your mother says that whipping you hurt her more than it hurt you, it is the way you cannot possibly see how it actually hurt her more than you, it is the way your siblings take care of you after you've been whipped since they know you've suffered greatly, it is the way ice cream melts in your hand since it's ninety-eight degrees outside, it is the way your knees are scraped after you fall off of a bike your grandfather is teaching you to ride, it is the way the pastor in a Baptist church that your grandmother wants to try out says he will let the church out in a few minutes but keeps us an hour longer with all of his hooting and hollering, it is the way your grandmother cuts her eyes at you for getting antsy in your seat when you realize the few minutes the pastor asked for have become almost an hour, it is the satisfaction you feel as a child when your tooth falls out and the tooth fairy is coming, it is the way that santa appears in the mall of your town and allows you to sit on his lap, it is the way you feel when you realize that your parents were the first people to lie to you all for the sake of tradition, it is the way your favorite teacher makes you feel at the end of the year when you are about to lose them forever, it is the way traffic is in the middle of the day, it is the way in which you dream of kissing a man who is of another race; it is the way a white man kisses you, it is the way a black man kisses you, it is the way you compare the ways in which they both kissed you, it is the way you feel ashamed that a white man kissed you in the first place, it is the way you compensate for being in love with that white man once upon a time during the summer of 2014 by

being the blackest person you know, it is the way you cannot
ever reveal how in love with this white man you actually
were/are, it is the way writing this poem could make you feel, it
is the way reading this poem made you feel, it is

                                                    the

                            way

        you

                                                                                 f

                                                                              eel.

love as some sort of sacerdotal relationship to God, if God were you

    Two decades into your life, I cannot imagine how difficult it must be to find yourself falling in love with a man who is five years and one month older than yourself.
    You fail to look me in the eyes when you speak. We have known each other for eight weeks now, and navigating anger is new for us. I grab your hand, and you pull away, try to walk away. I say your name softly but with a respectful aggression that asks that you respect me as well. Slowly, you walk back to me. You allow me to grab your hand, and I make sure that I caress every square inch of your hand. My touch exfoliates what roughness I feel upon that scoffed exterior.

> You felt like college. You felt like being in a new place without the knowledge of where to eat or where to meet new friends. You felt like finding a song that succinctly defines the emotion you are feeling that you had previously not been able to articulate.

    You are so young. You are so wise. You are so kind. You are so angry. You are understanding. You lack compassion. You remind me of someone I once knew, some familiar face my eyes have had the pleasure of seeing many autumns ago. There's a beauty in you that has not been raped, yet; hasn't been pillaged, yet; hasn't been infiltrated, yet. Please. Please, don't allow yourself to be a victim. I am dangerous. You can trust my fingers as they fervently explore the profundity of your face. You can trust my exhale as whispers float like steady winds upon the folds of your conscience. You can trust these eyes, the brown of them filled to the brim with brute honesty. But, you cannot trust that I will not break your heart. I can, and inevitably, I will. You are so kind. Don't allow me to change that. Must loss be included in our narrative?

        What happens to the mind when it cannot recover a lost memory, an experience that has passed and is gone? What happens to me when I cannot remember what it feels for your soul to reach out and caress mine? Will I weep? Will I call out your name, grimacing in how jagged the letters are as they cut away at my throat? It fucking hurts. My professor told me last semester that writing is cheapened with vulgarity. But, the word fucking is the best way to describe how much it hurts to lose someone.

this work was almost an epistolary novel

God,

My entire life I have harbored so much hatred against you founded upon the assumption that you were a man. I know that you are a woman.

the second time we made love

      He is a consummate artist. He paints my body with the tip of his brush, gently, lightly, erratically, the strokes define who he is as an individual.
      His avarice is unrivaled; his tongue attempts to discern the flavor of every atom of my body.
      His replies to my questions are made in silence; there is nothing that he says that I do not understand. He ensures that I do understand, neglecting a possibility that I could not understand. This is the deftness that he is capable of; an adroitness that is immeasurable by my standards.
      He strangles me and I gulp for air, being held down by his weight; it is not heavy but is balancing, a scale of sorts. This is a skill he has sharpened, penetrating in a way that isn't sharp or violent but confident and smooth.
      His fingers are upon my cheek. They walk, blithely but intentionally, upon the angles of my face.
      He smiles with his entire mouth, and I appreciate the way I can see every tooth.
      The length of his arms engulfs me, yet I breathe comfortably; oxygen has a softness to it that is intensely gratifying yet grounding. He provides such a feeling, a feeling that I cannot forget once he lets go of me and a feeling I cannot remember until he holds me. How does memory function in such illogicality?
      He holds my hand even when it is I who should be comforting him. Reciprocity is an apparent concept in every interaction he has with me. He takes his time. There are clocks in disrepair, and he is the source of their malfunction.
      I know his name, I call it out, it escapes my mouth and tastes delicious. I attempt to keep that flavor on my tongue, hide it within the confines of my cheeks.
      I say your name while you exhale and write words upon my walls that have not been touched before by man.

doughnuts and closets

There was a soft compassion in her eyes that morning, softer than usual. I didn't notice it at first since the sun insidiously permeated the crevices of my eyes as soon as they opened. Instead, it was when both pairs of our eyes were more accepting of the sun's harsh good-morning.

She made me put down both of the truck's visors while she firmly gripped the steering with both of her hands—hands that had encouraged, raised, nurtured, reprimanded, loved, and held six children and then all of their children.

So early in the day, the sun was eager to do its job. Her eyes went from squinting to smiling. Her hands relaxed. The steering wheel could finally breathe.

I could finally breathe.

Something was different. My grandmother didn't have favorites. There was no difference between any of the others and myself, even if her hands had held me first before any of them existed.

I was too short for the visor to do me any good. This was an old-school vehicle, its seats not particularly welcoming but accepting. Her truck, white with a maroon hood that was added on after a wreck two years prior, was made for super masculine and muscular cowboys, men who lived in Texas where they supposedly believed that bigger was better. I wasn't super masculine and muscular. I wasn't a cowboy. I doubted that I was a damn man. This was normal to ponder in my eighteen-year-old mind.

I could hear the squeal of the rubber that coated the steering wheel as her hands tensed up again.

We're going to get doughnuts, she said.

I couldn't decide if her voice burned like the early sunlight was burning my right arm as it hung out of the truck as we drove, struggling to collide with enough wind that would cool it down.

Okay, I said. I figured that was all I should say. Momo was a woman of many words, and her choice to utilize only five of them made me nervous.

You're not in trouble, she said. She knew her children and grandchildren very well.

I nodded suspiciously.

She continued, you're not in trouble, but I do want to know a few things.

I remained silent.

The truck's hum provided some irrelevant word that replaced the awkwardness that would have accompanied the silence.

When did you know? Her voice was almost timid. My grandmother, a woman whose gentle but violent stare could function as truth serum, seemed afraid of me.

Her question brushed against my body.

I allowed myself the opportunity to see if it would hurt. I waited several long seconds. There was no pain.

When did I know what, Momo?

When did you know you were different?

Her words were soft—had they been placed on paper, they were without quotation marks.

I realized this conversation was for her comfort, and not for mine. I recognized that. I had known that I was gay all of my life. But, this was the first time someone so critical, so powerful, so Christian was asking me directly. She was trying to come to terms with the idea. The processes were different, I guess.

Silence.

I took a breath. I just knew, I said. I just knew. Had I repeated myself in order to convince myself or her? It was the truth, but there was a nagging feeling that the truth was indeed the truth. This was the cognitive dissonance bullshit that a crazy professor had lectured about for two hours before I left his classroom and dropped the course. I knew I was gay—knew exactly what I was—but felt as though there were something wrong with existing. It was an internal struggle in the mind of an individual labeled as gay by society. I hadn't made the damn word up and painted on my own forehead. It was not of my own volition.

We were pulling up to the doughnut shop. I liked the scent of doughnuts. I held on to it, relishing in the fact that no matter how familiar it became it always appeared to be new. But, the scent wasn't inviting today.

The sun still burned my skin. Yet, I was shivering as if it were cold. My nerves were failing me. I wondered if my grandmother, this surveyor of black babies and children who played in a Louisiana yard with yellow grass and sturdy trees, had noticed.

The truck was parked, heavy and solemn like the mood.

Quez, she said lightly. She had turned her body toward me. Her tone was soft and inviting, and it sounded like the scent of doughnuts seeping out of crevices and cracks of the doughnut shop's building. I held onto it, soothed by it as I had been thousands of times as a child.

I looked into her eyes, slowly turning my body toward her as well.

I had forgotten about the doughnuts.

She spoke first. I love you, baby. The words rushed at me and hit me with the force of a friendly zephyr, invoking tears. It was a different type of crying; the tears fell indiscriminately. I felt no pain as each of them streaked across my cheek with unbridled freedom. I love you, she said again. I love you so much. Nothing will ever change that.

I love you too, Momo.

You can tell me anything.

I know.

I will always be here for you, God willing.

I know, Momo. And, I'll always be here for you.

She smiled. She was waiting. For what, I had no idea. We sat for a few moments in silence as the sun evaporated my precious tears.

Are you…? Are you in…? Are…?

I sighed. I knew what she was asking. I also knew what it meant to answer her questions. It hurt my body to formulate the answers, to form the words. Yes, I said.

We were next in line, the woman at the window explaining the prices to a man driving an old maroon minivan in front of us.

She smiled with even more zeal. Thank you for telling me, she said. Thank you for being yourself with me. You want any doughnuts, she asked.

Glazed, I said.

Okay. Glazed then, she said.

Black people don't need a therapist; we need a miracle, one not of God but of ourselves; we need help

The inclination to become more religious is what one could expect after a traumatic event in life; or, at least this is my experience. GOD IS A WOMAN is tattooed on the right side of my body with GOD beginning on my upper most rib and WOMAN ending up a few inches up from my waist. Two and a half hours in, I had already scrunched my shirt and placed a portion of it into my mouth so as to stop myself from screaming. The tattoo artist, an Asian man who had the glowing face of a Californian and the demeanor of a New Yorker or stern Louisianan grandmother, silently scoffed and pouted at the tension in my body. The pain taught me a lesson—God is a woman and I could not bear the burdens of the world that she has given birth to, much less a tattoo. I wasn't feeling religious when I had those words stained on my skin, and I hadn't felt exactly religious afterward.

Looking for myself in the mirror and seeing nothing allowed me to see God—to see myself, regardless of perceived vanity and blasphemy—and not some omniscient white robe-wearing white man sitting upon a golden throne that somehow defies gravity and rests on clouds that contain neither rain or snow. Heaven is not a cold place, or so says the Bible.

Peering into a mirror was almost recreational before he had broken me, my shattered persona indicative of my grasp of the world. The shattered mirror mirrored me.

It is religious now. I celebrate myself, comfortable sitting upon my altar and neglecting a humility that mortals should clamor to inherit. I am not a moral, I am God. Do I know come from her hips, having taken my first breath because of her will to carry me and deliver me into the world? Is she not amazing for being able to do this with every single human being who lives and exists?

But, not all of us see ourselves in the mirror and see God?

I do. It took losing myself to see who God truly is.

~~You~~ (I don't know you anymore) ~~were so angry that I had gotten that tattoo without you~~.
He was livid that I had gotten that tattoo without him.
And, I realized that his anger validated the reason these words mean so much to me: men who are threatened become your enemy and God cannot ever be threatened.
You displayed your mortality in that moment, and I never forgot it.

black lives matter in coffee shops, too

I am about to leave Austin, Texas and I've decided to take a second, catch my breath. As I inhale the nauseous, yet comforting scent of Arabica coffee beans, I realize I'm surrounded by white people. They love Starbucks.

But, what do I love?

I shrug off the burden of that question, my mind choosing to ignore that I don't have the answer.

Yellow lined notebook paper. Cheap blue pen. I wrote him a note this morning before I left the apartment we had shared for the past two days. There were smiles, laughs, card games, and showers together. There was lying in bed, love-making, deep conversation, trust, a divulging of life choices.

The note said:

Ron,

I have thoroughly enjoyed the past two days with you as we have gotten to know each other better. Thank you for opening up and sharing a small part of you with me. I'll see you later, OK?

What was it about him that caused me to feel so comfortable?

I inhale again and don't smell the Starbucks full of white patrons. Instead, I am breathing in the scent of his neck seemingly doused in woodsy cologne, his body lathered with Old Spice soap, his torso freshly washed and natural—it smells of salty water that is ensnaring and perilous to drink.

He was charming, and he knew that I was aware of that. He was kind and compassionate. He was witty. He was sarcastic. He was accepting.

The coffee hurts my stomach. Do I need to drink any to make it stop? I look behind me and a white woman with obviously dyed red hair wearing a bright purple shirt looks my way. I sheepishly break eye contact. She seems to know that I have spent the last two days making love to a man who is not the man I am in love with. I feel as though she will tell Jerome. Do I want him to know? Should I tell him everything?

Three years. Throw that all away?

I rationalize my mistake—no, my choice. This was not a mistake. Ron was not a simple mistake. What we shared was not a mistake. I chose to taste him—all of him.

Lying to protect someone is rationalization.

At least, that's what I tell myself.

After making love last night, I had asked him to wake me up when he had to leave for work. He assured me that he would, delivering gentle kisses to my back and hips. We slept in each other's embrace, the strong oscillating fan obliterating any body heat that would have caused us to become uncomfortable.

A few taps to the shoulder woke me a few hours later and I peered up at him as he stood over me, his stance full of power but radiating of admiration and absent of intimidation. My body was still inundated with fatigue.

I sat up in his bed to be closer to this man I didn't know much about.

Don't get up for me. I'm about to leave, he said.

We hugged, my arms didn't want to leave his waist. We let go.

He smiled.

Two hours later I awoke, aware that I would be leaving him and our apartment behind to go back to my boyfriend and my apartment. In the shower, I brushed my teeth and washed my face silently. I didn't want to reflect, I wanted to be empty of everything. Goodbyes were never good for me. I grabbed my suitcase and my pillow and used the key he had given me the day before to lock the door. I then placed it at the top of the door's frame, hoping no one would be smart enough to look up there and break into his space. Driving away from his apartment was easy enough. The guilt that trailed me all the way back to Houston couldn't be described as such.

***

I tried ignoring it. I attempted to mimic Jerome and the sleep that had him in a lovely coma, but my thoughts transformed into a monstrosity, a metallic spider with glistening sharp legs that stretched and grew and touched everything. It was 3 AM. I was awake.

Did he read the note I left him?
Was I too forward?
Why am I thinking of another man when Jerome is lying beside me, peacefully sleeping?
Why can't I sleep?
Is it the guilt?
Is it because I feel stupid leaving him a note that basically expresses that I care about him?
Did I say those words last night?
Did I say: I CARE ABOUT YOU, RON?
I think I fucking did.
What's wrong with me?
I'm greedy.
I'm an avaricious monster who wants what he can't have.
Did we...

I lie in silence, my eyes fluttering and shrieking, making noise that vibrates throughout my body. They see things. They *make* me see things. And feel things. And hear things. And remember things. It's a beautiful, painful agony. I crave to be Tiresias, blind to what the world really looks like.

I get out of bed, silently. I don't like to wake Jerome when he's so content with the world, at peace with society and himself as his wildest dreams vividly come to fruition. His head is the only safe space for him these days. I am dangerous; there's no safe space inside of me for him at the moment.

My last thought allows me to realize I am indeed selfish—spitefully so.

I sit here, thinking, wondering. I sit here in the lonely living room that Jerome and share in our small, unattractive apartment. I contemplate my life choices and who I am, though the past cannot be changed. I guess I think about these choices to make a decision regarding whether or not I will regret them. Mostly, there is no regret but instead an attempt to cleanse myself with cheap lemon tea and generic rice cakes lightly brushed with honey that I choose not to put into my tea.

I don't know anymore—about life and everything that is, but I'm ok with that. I am learning that I am not as naive and innocent as I previously thought myself to be. I'm an asshole—a loving one at that—but more importantly I am someone who is young and upset with the world and the circumstances I am not able to control. In this place of powerlessness, I am seeking to find a variable that bends to my hand—one that I can manipulate and steer. Is this wrong? Is it so horrible that I want to be significant that I will do whatever it takes to maintain that feeling? Is it wrong that I want the thrill of another man who doesn't know me as well as Jerome? Is it wrong that I kiss this new person with a voracious admiration for his lips that taste of caramel and his neck that smells of primrose and his back stained with black ink and his shoulders made of rock? Is it wrong wanting to then return home and make love to Jerome like I've never made love to him? Am I a bitch? Am I a monster?

I pondered that question as I sat upon this new man's couch in his living room, the room we have played card games and watched movies in during these last two days I escaped to meet him here in Austin. I peered into the bedroom, the one in which I told him I would not fuck, but instead would make love. The bed called to me, beckoning with invisible and crafty fingers. I paused and felt the gentle force of him entering me from behind, his breath in my ear and upon my cheek as he rocked himself to sleep. I am a lullaby. I am a bedtime story. I am what he has always wished he could have. He was my fantasy and a man whose existence will die along with my body as I take my last breath when I am almost 100 years old.

This is what sex with a stranger feels like.

He never spoke to me again.

I ain't got shit [November 2017]

I had to go to Japan to find some shit for myself.

Some of my life—new pieces of it.
Starting over from the life you stole.
You came in with used Wal-Mart bags and loaded up on merchandise.
My life.
Nobody checked your receipt at the doors even though you had stolen all of my shit.
Literally walked off with all of my shit.
And left me with nothing to my name; not a dollar or a damn dream.
I had spent all my money on you; gave you all of my life—every single thing I had to offer—without so much as a thought.
I didn't hesitate because I was taught that's what you do in love.
You are selfless, you give all of yourself, you don't question anything.
And, you walked right out of my life with all of my shit.
My shit.
The shit I had gathered and collected my entire life; gone in one day.
The day you decided to take your trifling ass to another place, another store, another man.
I had invested so much into your stocks.
So much into your value.
So much into who you were as an individual.
So much that I took out loans because I didn't have enough of myself left to give anymore.
Ain't that some shit?
My life and other people's lives that I borrowed.
All gone in one day.

When your ass decided loving me was too expensive.
Shit, you had drained all I had and asked for more.
I took life from another man to give to you.
I stole his shit and gave it all to you.
My shit.
His shit.
Your shit.
I never saw your shit.
I didn't realize you hadn't given me anything until I tried to cash a check at the bank.
And they turned my trifling ass around.
Ain't that some shit?
I was on top of the world with all of my shit.
Tried to be muthafucking philanthropic and you ran off with all of my shit.
My life.
How in the fuck do I get my shit back?
I can't file a police report because I'm tired of their shit and America's shit.
My shit took a long time to be my shit.
And, in a day you took my life.
It ain't murder because I'm alive.
But, I'm not breathing.
I'm not eating.
I'm not drinking.
I'm not running.
I'm not reading.
I'm not existing.
I ain't shit since you took all of my shit.

harry with the small blue truck who smelled like cigarettes—Kool

I thought that allowing
a white man to rape me
would spare my sister
but he infiltrated her mind
and destroyed her imagination
she was never able to cultivate
seeds of a childhood's beautiful future in her mind,
and instead,
cultivated his.

Black oil

[*In Lake Charles, Louisiana sometime in 1997*]
Want to know what happens when five children see a can of black oil? Want to know how quickly a white porch can be covered with handprints? Want to know how surprised my grandmother was to see our art? Want to know when I ever touched a can of oil again?

#2 does not exist

#1 came into my life early summer and had broken me by the onset of fall.

He's the reason I sit for six hours
on the couch
without once blinking or breathing or perceiving.
I feel empty, spent, used.

It's the fake Swarovski crystal bracelet that helps me remember that he was at all even real. I have to tell myself that someone gave that to me—someone who cared once upon a time. Yes, he was a man I was in love with.

He was the first man that I ever begged to love me. I felt ashamed.

I made this mistake again several months later when the man I then begged was my brother.

He was the last.

$13.27 for a moment of security

I buy flowers and lunch
for myself now.
The grass grows
despite it encountering sharp blades
every single Saturday.

We forgot how to be environmentalists once they broke our hearts

we picked wish flowers—dandelions—
as children
blew its seeds away with a buoyant exhalation
and wished for things, for people
for money to turn on the electricity
for our fathers to love us
for the lives of white kids on television
for cheese that wasn't block-shaped
    or reminiscent of brick and mortar
for church clothes that hadn't been worn already by the Protestants
    or anybody
for gas money to get to the other side of town to see our grandmother
for anyone to understand that we were more than
mulatto children who did not belong in the 'hood
mulatto children playing outside with sticks and branches
mulatto children who played games with imagination
mulatto children who explored the forest near us
mulatto children who could swim in the river in that forest
mulatto children who had a turkey and a huge box of food for the rest of the year
    delivered on Thanksgiving
mulatto children who had their home broken into many times
mulatto children who could not beg for anything
    lest they desired the fury of a woman
    lighter and brighter than them
    but who had five children by the age of twenty-three
    and knew everything about using an intelligence on the streets

and nothing about using it within the space created by four walls

numbers like 24

six is such an arbitrary number
and abs aren't beautiful anymore
since I neglected the membership.
I consume cookies and ice cream
and my stomach hurts.
finally, I can feel
something
since you broke my heart
at the gym.

you in a royal blue T-shirt

on my cell, there is a recording of your laugh.
I deleted it yesterday and cried myself to sleep.
oranges mold in a glass bowl
on the glass table
of the dining room.
where is the zest?
why do they taste bland
since you stole my joy
for the most beautiful color?

i hate you

a bird, a gorgeous black bird,
told me you are back in college.
how can I know you in the nude?—
know your body's dimensions?—
know how every part of you tastes?—
yet
not know your major?
am I not your best friend
or was that a lie too?

five months

five months.
that is how long
it takes to sap every ounce
of willingness to love another
from the blood of a previous lover.
october 19.
I don't bother at blood drives.
no amount of glucose in the snack cakes helps.
they don't want the blood of gay men anyway.
I hate you
and
honey mustard
and
chicken
and
cranberry juice.

She tells me losing you was the equivalent of losing air in my lungs and it's the fucking truth

    therapy isn't so fucking pretty
    when you don't want to cry   won't cry   shouldn't cry
    but you fucking cry.
    and my therapist peers into my exposed soul
    and I dislike that even after you made off
    with every single good thing I had
    that I am still open for business and vulnerable
    as if I haven't learned what it feels like
    to be the most intelligent person
    and fall prey to a cunningness and foolishness
    of a child.

I'm not a white, rich man so I don't have a solution

    being homeless is unhealthy and leads to mental health problems but
    I don't have a home because my home was you.

vw

every black car
could be you
so I slow down and shrink,
afraid that you'll see
that I have not yet attained
the refreshed glow brought on
by loving another.
as a child
I did not have the privilege
of losing a balloon
and having my tears dried with an even prettier balloon
because you were my only balloon to lose.
for the thousandth time
I have begged the sky for sympathy
and again, am met with a blue unmoving.

don't get it

men are so stupid.
your mother taught you how to love
when she carried you in her body
and shared her soul with a being
she knew would eventually
deny her equal rights   equal pay   equal freedom.
you take   take   take
when all she did was give   give   give
but scoff at her trying to be more like you.

on a Thursday? —the same day you threw me away?

when we made love
we never did.
on what day did you declare
to God
that you had fallen out of love with me?
don't worry I am pissed at her too.
language acquisition + anger = but;
three-word statements have now become six.
I love you becomes *I love you but fuck you*
I miss you becomes *I miss you but fuck you*
my therapist smiles,
says *fuck* is a good word
a healing word
says she is proud of me
but *fuck*
does nothing for me
when I see you at our favorite bar
and I have to pull over since my wailing won't allow me to drive home.
    the last time we made love
there lacked an empathy in your eyes
as if each thrust was supposed to hurt
so I closed my eyes and tried to feel you
but that man was not you.
I did not feel a man with compassion, understanding, discernment—
what I felt was selfishness, pain, foreshadowing—
you leaving me filthy as you entered the shower alone
I lay in bed waiting on a
come join me, my love
come here, baby
I need you in here now
but I only heard the water on your skin
until you turned it off

and told me I had to go.

philanthropy

I'd give back my iPhone for you
trade in both of my dogs
renounce my citizenship
cut off an arm
become religious
dance in poison ivy
live on an island
wash your feet daily with rosewater
and yet even then
you still wouldn't want to be with me.

no fried chicken

I.

No fried chicken, no Kool-Aid, no watermelon because we are not them, my mother said sternly.

That's what she said to all of us in the canned goods aisle of Wal-Mart when we wanted to be black one day. We paid attention to her words carefully, taking in all 5'2" of her thick body. The women in my family were never skinny. That day I had likened her complexion to the color of condensed milk.

Easy for her to tell us how not to be black when she didn't look black.

But how are we supposed to not be black, we had asked her infrequently or so for almost ten years after that. We never received an answer. Mostly, we were taught how *not* to be black.

—*Don't ever curse in front of white people, always say please and thank you in a high pitched voice so that white people aren't scared of you, never take the last of anything left on a plate because you'll look greedy and white people don't like greedy people, always try to learn what you can from them by watching, don't let white people catch you watching them, just sit and listen to how they speak, I'll kill all any of you if you ever say 'ain't' or 'fo' or 'do,' the correct way to say all of them is 'isn't' and 'four' and 'door'. Ok,* she asked.

This memory and her scolding stalked my conscience as I stood in line behind the other starving freshman at Grambling State University. It was my first time in a college cafeteria; it was my first time anywhere on a college campus really.

There had been no college tours, no visiting out-of-state campuses, no making a tough decision about where I would spend the next four years of my life. My mother didn't know what FAFSA, or financial aid, was. My high school counselor, who had taken a liking to me, had paid my college application fee and helped me fill it out without consulting my mother. Mrs. Weston, a rebellious, heavyset black woman liked to break the rules if she had a reason to do so. She had told me multiple times that I could not be the smart black boy who became a statistic by circumstance. She told me this in her office as I ate candy and food she had bought from home. Many times, she would call me out of class just to check on me and ask me if I had eaten that day. It was encouragement and love she wanted to give me. Her words sounded like poetry, a poetry that I cared nothing for and failed to understand at the time.

This food smells good as hell, said a caramel-colored girl with long, jet black braids swept into a sleek ponytail. A few girls behind her agreed. People were making friends quickly. It fascinated me—how black people could just fit in and begin anew in any environment. I felt like I hadn't been taught how to do that. I had been taught to fit into a world of white. But, this was a world of blackness.

Our line was advancing pretty quickly, and we were almost at the front desks where two cafeteria women scanned our school IDs and allowed us to eat everything that blackness could cook and bake: heavily-seasoned hamburgers, Cajun chicken and rice, beef stir-fry, meat pies, peach cobbler, sweet potato pie, fried fish. I could smell and see it all. Finally, after being scanned in, I walked into a massive room that seemed to comfortably hold every student on campus. There were circular tables that could seat up to eight people, square tables for four, and private tables for one or two. I emulated what I saw upperclassmen do and placed my school ID on the table I wanted, a table for one.

After visiting only a few sections of the cafeteria, I had already hastily grabbed an entire plate of food. The experience was glorious. I could feel the potatoes in the sweet potato pie. I could hear the peaches in the peach cobbler. I could smell the Cajun in the Cajun chicken and rice. My grandmother had always said people could do at least one thing right in life. It was the thing they were created to do. I had definitely found out what the black people in this Northern Louisiana university's cafeteria could do: cook.

The food wasn't enough to console me when I was attacked with the sense of being misplaced, being kept somewhere strange and impractical. I used my roommate's cell phone later that night to call my mom and grieve. I walked outside and sat outside on the curb of one of our main streets.
I cannot stay here, I said.
What's wrong, she asked.
They're all black, I responded.
Give it some time, she said.
Time for what? Time for them to hate me more than they already do? Time for them to call me a white boy again? Time for them to tell me that I'm too smart and that it's annoying that I pretend to know everything? My voice had grown to a high pitch and students walking nearby had begun to look at me.
Calm down. Don't worry about anybody else except you. Just do what you have to do to get me my house and car that you promised, she said.
I smiled. I love you, I said.
I love you, too, she said.
We hung up.
I thanked Jarvis for allowing me to use his phone. He didn't respond with a you're welcome. I felt slighted. Black people were so weird.
I slept with my wallet underneath my pillow just in case Jarvis turned out to be the worst of the black stereotypes: a thief.

In the school celebrations that followed during freshman orientation, I felt out of place. My bleach-stained Chuck Taylors, Salvation Army graphic tee shirt, and Wal-Mart skinny jeans were stark contrasts to my peers' black and red Jordan's, basketball jerseys, and True Religion baggy jeans. I felt white. I felt gay.
I cried every night for two weeks.

II.

It is in these moments that my memories harass me. I am reading or meditating or eating. The quiet; the silent; the tranquil.

As I sit at my dining room table eating tomato soup, I realize I don't love the man who is supposed to be my father. I picture his face, a conglomerate of contorted expressions: anger, disappointment, disgust, denial, cynicism. Those are the gifts my father offers to his son. I smell the disappointment that he offers me.

I know that my father is the beginning of my slippery slope with black men.

The past attacks me.

That all-too-familiar scent of cheap beer was on his breath and in his dingy white T-shirt and in his worn black jeans. We sat in the garage, in the old house he and my stepmother lived in before they moved to the new house with a backyard. I hated the garage. I hated Gabriel Dwayne Watkins. I hated being with him.

We never talked as father and son. We didn't know how to accomplish such a feat. What kind of man enters his son's life when he's twelve? He had only known me for about six summers (one of which I refused to spend with him), which is a long time if a person is a friend. But, this was my father and six years was an embarrassment. At least, it was an embarrassment for me.

The past attacks me.

We would stand in line in a grocery store, like the bright and lively but uncomfortable Fiesta, waiting on our turn to check out. The cashier would say hello and he would nervously chuckle, say hello back, and say something awkward:

We are going to cook up some fish and make a meal together; father and son, he would say.

But I don't eat seafood, I would say.

The cashier would decide that what was happening wasn't her business, focusing keenly on scanning everything as quickly as she could.

Another nervous chuckle left his mouth.

He showed me time and time again that he didn't know anything about me; not my favorite color, favorite food, what I liked or disliked, what I was allergic to, nothing.

That pervasive, nervous chuckle would announce itself and I wanted to scream.

The air in the garage was hot and stifling, an indicator that hell was sure to ensue. Maybe it was the junk in it. Maybe it was the tension between us. I prayed a little. To God: her, him, it. I prayed to something. I choked a little and cleared my throat.

His accusatory dark brown eyes remained on the television.

I have my mother's eyes. I wanted to have more from her and less from him—this mime of a man who could never express what he wanted to say except through critical and sharp eyes.

Maybe he wanted to look at me but needed a reason to. He didn't believe in exerting energy for the sake of emotions. In fact, he seemed emotionless.

I have something to tell you, I said.

What? He looked at me then.

Well, I found out something about myself. Well, I've been knowing for a long…I don't know what to say.

What? He looked annoyed.

I'm gay, I said. The words wounded my chest as they fluttered away, breaking free from my rib cage. But this was the good kind of pain—the pain you have to sometimes experience in order to feel better. At eighteen years old, I felt released; my feelings were no longer insidious shadows hidden from plain sight.

You're what, he asked. I wondered if his words formed a rhetorical question.

We sat in silence for about five minutes before he left the garage and entered the house. My stepmother soon walked out and sat next to me. She looked me in the eyes and held my left hand in hers.

She spoke meekly, but forcefully. I've called your mom already. She's on the way from Lake Charles. Why didn't you wait, Quez? Why couldn't you hide it for a little longer?

We sat there, listening to the passing cars for two hours before Angel pulled up in her gold Hyundai Elantra.

During our ride home, I told my mother everything that happened.

This is why I didn't want him to come back into your life, she said.

I sat there in the lonely passenger seat; saying nothing; looking through her; feeling empty.

He's a sorry excuse for a black man, she continued, and I am so sorry he is what you were stuck with. She didn't use the word 'who' but used the word 'what'. It was as if we were both aware he was a monster.

A father isn't supposed to do that to his child, I say.

Quez—she began.

I hate him. I hate black men. I hate black people. I meant every single word that left the confines of my mouth. This statement was not as freeing as the one that announced my sexual orientation, albeit the sayer of it never having had sex before.

She sat there, focusing on the road but taking a few chances to look at me sympathetically.

I realized that we were the same. Black men had ridiculed us, hurt us, and abandoned us.

The past attacks me once again.

I was a fifteen-year-old in a LaGrange Senior High School classroom with brick walls that were painted off-white. The walls are a stark contrast to the shades of black that stain the skin of students all around me. This was a black school; one that taught me so many things including ways in which I *could* hate myself.

    A hideously drawn periodic table poster overwhelmed the wall to my right. I sat next to that poster and the window it halfway covered. I wore a navy-blue shirt and khaki shorts, the same as my other thirty or so classmates. Our chemistry teacher and my favorite teacher, Mrs. Reed, had left the room for a moment. She had asked if she could trust us before leaving out. Half of the room answered. The other half patiently anticipated an opportunity like starving lions.

    I sneezed. I regretted making any noise and ceasing to be invisible.

    Don't get your gay germs on us, Keilon's raspy voice exclaimed. A few laughs followed his statement.

    I looked at him and quickly analyzed him. About 5'7, complexion similar to coffee with no cream and three sugars, 185 pounds, goofy-looking, insecure.

    Don't worry about me, I replied. I didn't enjoy confrontation, but I was quick-witted and stubborn. He could have a fight if he wanted.

    Stop looking at me while we are getting dressed in the gym, he said.

    I don't watch you, I said.

    I see you looking at me, John, Josh, Devin. All of the basketball players, he said. He pointed to our classmates as he spoke.

    They began to talk amongst themselves.

    I'll kill you if I see you watching me, one of them said. Maybe it was John. My face was burning from an unintentional mortification. I hated that I didn't want to give him power, but his words became truth as this is how bullying works.

    I don't watch anyone, I said.

    Those words were meant for all of them, every single person in the classroom who was either laughing at me or not defending me. I felt all of their eyes. The girls in the corner who wore heavy makeup. They didn't say "stop" or "leave him alone". The nerds who were grouped together in the front continued to sit there quietly. There was no other gay kid to defend me, protect me, stick up for me.

Faggot, one of them said.

The snickers and giggles slowly died as Mrs. Reed's footsteps grew louder and louder. She entered the classroom with a smile.

Are we ready to continue learning about magnesium? Mrs. Reed was not even aware that a student had died in her classroom, the stench of it invisible to adults who assumed we couldn't be as ruthless as they were.

III.

High school in 1990 was supposed to be abnormal shapes in geometry, rhetorical devices in English, and trivial betrayals in history that would cease to matter after graduation, a particularly defining moment that Angel Marie Jackson would not see until almost seven years later when she received her GED. Instead, high school was a lesson in which she learned that love was a burden; a collection of costly bags that held a heaviness incapable of being quantified. At fifteen years old, Angel Marie Jackson did not expect to become pregnant. Along with the growth of her notoriety as the freshman light-skinned black girl with white girl's hair, her belly grew exponentially. She would begin her high school career without a care in the world and end it a year later craving everything that the world's crudeness makes one want to crave.

I was born early evening at 7:23 PM on a Wednesday of June 1991. My family was there to receive me—all one of them. The other half of my parents had already abandoned us seven months earlier.

My father, the first man—the first black man—that my mother had ever loved, disappeared and never returned.

After the birth of my mother's first child, me, the responsibilities that came along with me and the absence of my father's existence proved too much for her. My young grandmother, who had given birth to my mother at fifteen years old, provided as much support as she could. Again, a black man appeared at Angel's doorstep once again in a thunderstorm with the lure of happiness and gifts. She heartily accepted all of that heaviness, adding to the load she was already carrying.

Two years later, Estevez came into the world, grasping in his tiny hands a gift for our mother: postpartum depression.

She was different. How could she not be? My brother and I spent a lot of time with my grandmother. I don't think my mother understood what she was feeling, and it affected her in every aspect of life—her weight, her appetite, her ambition. She tried to find herself in men and the love they could provide.

A year later, Enistazha appeared along with trauma from the rape that created her. Love kept bringing its gifts. The second black man that she had later fallen in love with, yearning for freedom, disappeared into the world.

She had lost another man, one that had raped her and created his second child with her. Hurt, she became reclusive and didn't want to live anymore. Yet, she persevered.

Love, relentless in his courting of a woman who had had enough, arrived at our doorstep. Our three young faces shone with curiosity when he presented more baggage; a convicted felon, June, who proposed and eventually married her was a precursor to the two rambunctious children, Estevon and Azhia, that completed the bunch. My grandmother, burdened with helping my mother's five younger siblings and their spiraling lives, couldn't do much to help with my siblings and I—five children and several pounds of headache.

A marriage to a man who despised the children that were not biologically his and embraced infidelity with a greediness that could not be contained drained her. She worked three jobs to keep food on the table, cigarettes in June's violent tattooed hands, and her sanity in check. She cried often. She didn't eat. She couldn't sleep. Yet, she worked.

As a young woman, Angel wished that she could give back what the world had forcibly thrust at her. At the age of twenty-five, she finally began to ignore love and his empty promises of better gifts, expensive baggage that cost her more than money.

I didn't know how my mother looked or what her laugh sounded like or what foods she liked to cook, mostly because the bags and their contents had buried her. Love, a deformed and evil figure of blackness, had betrayed and degraded her. It was then that she decided to refuse blackness. And, as her children, we were made to share the same sentiments.

Working is what made her feel important, so that is what she poured her entire self into. She shirked her responsibilities as wife, mother, and father.

I was eight years old when I became a wife, mother, and father. My newly acquired husband *and* child was 6'3", the shade of an adobe-colored Native American. June was thoroughly less impressed with a scrawny child who had to balance third grade with homemaking duties. As a twenty-six-year-old high school dropout and drunk, he had figured he and my mother would make the perfect couple. But, she was evading life's responsibilities through her menial jobs while he sat at our house watching television and smoking countless cigarettes, seemingly trying to find his life's purpose within them.

I learned how to clean through the process of vicious verbal and physical lashings from June. My tears and pain transformed an untidy, dark, cramped house into a home for my siblings and me. It was never a home for my mother because she was never there. It was never a home for June because he was never satisfied with the work of his new wife.

I learned how to cook by having bowls of food thrown at my head by my stepfather and siblings, alike. Variations of overly-seasoned Ramen noodles and bologna sandwiches became lasagna, spaghetti, gumbo, beef tips with yellow rice, and other dishes that were consumed with only the sound of silence. Empty bowls meant I was doing a decent job.

My marriage to my mother's cheating, unemployed husband was comprised of hatred. On his drunken nights, he cursed at me for not being able to make her come home. I don't think the alcohol ever allowed him to realize that she didn't want to be home.

We divorced him six years later; all of us attaining freedom from a leech that was sucking the souls from our bodies. Another black man disappeared into the world and never looked back at the children and ex-wife he left behind.

With that freedom, Angel dropped most of the bags that held her down like enormous boulders. And then *that* freedom allowed her to move, to run, to fly. She did all of that—and did it vociferously.

I then transitioned into a husband to my mother. I continued living as a father—I knew that my siblings would remain as my children until they grew into adults.

My mother, aware that a fourteen-year-old was capable of raising her children, decided that life was now to be lived. She dated men who never met us, spent nights at places we never visited, and ate food that we had no idea existed. She was living her life as a white woman with black woman abilities. She was a novelty for the white men who wanted a companion. She was an exotic trophy for black men who wanted a thrill. She was a form of artistic expression for others.

Yet, they—all of them—were tools for her. She indiscriminately utilized them to fix her life and lighten her load. With the use of each one, she abandoned painful luggage that life had once gifted her with. At once, she was a fiancée to three different men.

While I was trapped in the realization that my life would probably be filled with fatherly responsibilities, my mother was in the midst of a realization that her smile and hair and existence could be used as currency in exchange for money, companionship, and *good* gifts. We both began to forget who the other was. Angel became my wife—a horrible one—and I became her best friend. I lost my mother and she lost her son.

I thought I had become one of the black men she used.

I used her as motivation to become the first high school graduate of my family.

My transition into college several months later came as a surprise for her. I told her I was leaving one week before I did. August of 2009, scorching and fiery, was the month my life changed forever. With a heavy heart full to the brim with guilt, I abandoned all of my responsibilities just as she had done for most of my life. I allowed her to be a mother for the first time in years. And, I allowed myself the privilege of being alone. Like the black men before me who had abandoned her disappeared into the world, I followed suit. I became the men I had yearned to not embody for so long.

You're leaving me, she asked. The question was definitely accusatory.

Ma, I have to buy you a house one day. Don't you want your own new car, I asked.

But, how?

Ma, college just happened. And, it's going to be great for all of us. Ok?

But, how did *it* just happen?

I filled out the FAFSA and got financial aid.

What's the FAFSA?

Ma, it's what the government calls the application for money to go to college. You don't sound happy for me.

Of course, I'm happy for you.

Thank you, Ma. I began packing again.

I'm going to miss you. She placed her arms around my shoulders from behind as I folding my only pair of denim jeans.

I stood there and just enjoyed that moment. I loved my mother more than any other human being on earth.

Quez, I know you have to go, but don't leave me.

I won't, Ma. I had turned around and hugged her the normal way.

And, you better call every day. I'll need help, she said.

I nodded and kissed her forcefully on the cheek. I always wanted her to *know* that her children loved her.

She giggled. It was a sound that my siblings and I loved to hear; we were the human beings that possessed the propensity to make her happy when everyone else in her life had only caused her pain.

Years later, I seemed to be the only one whose agenda included concern for her happiness.

She missed me dearly. Though, I could not discern if she missed her son or her husband and co-parent. We talked on the phone often. I always thanked Khadija, my best friend in college, for never complaining about how much her phone was actually in my hands and not hers.

Angel always sounded like she needed my help raising my younger siblings during our phone calls.

Why is Enistazha acting out like this, she asked me.

What is she doing, I asked. I had to maintain calmness in my tone in order to calm her. My mother was easily rattled.

She's sneaking out of the house to talk to boys at night and God knows what else. I'm going to kill her if I catch her again. I was fifteen when boys were whispering in my ear. I became pregnant with you.

Ma, she's fifteen. She wants to rebel. That's normal for people her age, I said.

I can't deal with it, she said.

Just give her more opportunities to feel more involved. Let her choose her responsibilities off of the list I made and left for you. She likes cooking.

Oh.

—I can't deal with *this*—the students, the professors, the black people who say I'm not black enough. My tone was panicked now. It was my turn to vent.

She sighed. She understood the problem I was having.

I don't know if I can do it, Ma. I was exasperated.

Just treat college like a man. Use him for everything he has, she said.

During my freshman year of college, I told her that I was gay.

What took so damn long? I was waiting on you, she exclaimed before wrapping her strong arms around me and gently squeezing all of the air out of my body.

Ma, I can't breathe, I said half-smiling, half-dying.

She let me go and we cried together.

I figured that telling my father next would be as easy. I decided that I would tell him a month later when I visited Houston.

I graduated from college using her advice. Sometimes I feel as though her influence had helped me become a monster. Every two weeks or so of my college career, I received a letter that read something inspirational and simple like, *You can do it* or *I believe in you, Quez* or *You are my favorite college student in the world*. I thought they were gifts from her that stemmed from her guilt of not being a mother to me or the gifts that she wished life would have given her instead of five children and a lifetime of problems. I never blamed her. I always smiled when reading them.

wanting a father eventually goes away ... until you drink too much

I am younger than I think I am. I crave the acknowledgement of a man who helped to conceive me almost 27 years ago.

No resuscitation, no CPR, no answers—losing yourself to the reality that the man you were about to leave your partner of four and a half years has decided to, in fact, leave you

I watched a documentary about the lives and deaths of trans women on the fifth day, ate handfuls of cereal out of the box with no milk and no hand sanitizer that would wash away the stickiness of colorful marshmallows, listened to music that made me cry, questioned my validity as a man, questioned my validity as a gay man, questioned my validity as a gay black man, questioned my validity as a human being who thought that I lived because of you, sat in the shower for six hours since standing meant being brave and I didn't know how to define courage in that moment, contemplated how I would afford the water bill next month, examined my fingers and how shriveled they looked, refused to wash the dishes for three days, drank ginger ale when a relentless need to vomit would present itself, marveled at the skins of oranges and how their zests tainted my fingers with a scent that only antibacterial soap could get rid of, walked the dogs, cursed at God as I walked the dogs, didn't ask for her forgiveness because I knew she understood exactly how a black man uses you all up and leaves you behind, didn't pick up my dogs' poop and instead relished in knowing someone would have to deal with shit that I refused to handle, cried when I realized that the shit in my life was heavier than dog's shit, looked in the mirror and cried some more at the ugliness of human nature and my weaknesses, gazed at myself lovingly, told myself that I was amazing and great and sexy and intelligent and everything else that I felt when I *was* loved by you, analyzed if you had ever loved me in the first place since love doesn't feel like abandonment and having to incessantly gasp for air as if you were breathing through the butt of a wet cigarette that is your only source of oxygen, promised a friend who lived five minutes away that I would bring over my vacuum since he needed it, didn't feel guilty that I passed up his house and drove six miles further for Chinese takeout, returned home with my vacuum in my backseat, smiled when I realized I had to keep some of my shit for myself rather than always allowing people to walk off with *my* shit, burnt frozen garlic bread and scraped it off since things that are a little abused seem to shine better than things that glitter like gold, put in my two weeks' notice before finding another job, interviewed for my dream job two days after that, got a call informing me that I didn't get that dream job, couldn't rescind my two weeks' notice, packed up the belongings in my office including a bamboo plant that was a hassle to get home without spilling water and took them home with me, left those belongings except the bamboo plant in the backseat of my car along with that damn vacuum, covered my bedroom window with a blue cover that causes my skin to itch and was probably purchased by an old woman at a not-so-reputable garage sale, slept in longer than I usually do, missed calls from bill collectors that would have woken me up, didn't use wash towels in the shower and instead rubbed the soap against my bare wet skin in an attempt to clean the shit in my life off of myself, lay across the bed and studied how the ceiling fan's blades seamlessly bled into each other, got a headache from trying to observe such a phenomenon, texted people I love and told them they are amazing and that I appreciate them, ignored every response text because I didn't need the validation, ran three miles without a shirt on, laughed at the people who looked at my body with what I perceived to be jealousy since that was the only emotion I wanted people to feel when they saw my body, slept naked and wore underwear only when I left the apartment, went to Wal-Mart and bought fruits that I knew I wouldn't eat in one day, lit cheap candles that only gave off the faintest light in a pitch black room, prayed to God only once and didn't feel bad when I watched porn instead of praying some more, felt ashamed at my selfishness, wallowed in failure, felt empowered by my selfishness, slept every night with a box fan that kissed my face with cold air and made me numb, wrote a letter to my grandmother, googled ways to kill myself without hurting those that love me, laughed at the notion that another human being could bring me to that point, drank a glass of wine and came to my senses, deleted two pictures of you from my phone, saved five pictures of you from my phone so that I could one day look at your face and not feel any emotion whatsoever, cooked spaghetti and used ground turkey instead of ground beef, attended class and barely passed my midterm, doubted the usefulness of my Master's program, ate three bananas in less than two minutes and chuckled at how silly and great it felt to be achieving and not losing, met a friend for coffee and ordered a small latte with 4 sugars and 2 creams, decided to drink a gallon of water throughout the day for the sake of accomplishing a goal, boiled five eggs and stood over the stove until they cooled and then peeled them with fingers that had wiped tears from my eyes for eight days and nights straight, cackled at videos of babies eating lemons for the first time, ate ice cream and prepared for zits to appear on my face in the next few days, drank tea with no lemon or sugar but only a little honey, asked God why women are the only positive beings in my life, asked God why I am gay, asked God why I met the person who had decided to break my heart, called my ex-boyfriend and asked him what it felt like to have his heart be broken by me a couple of years prior, looked at the pictures of you and wondered why I hadn't deleted them yet, typed three-fourths of this poem and tossed and turned while trying to get sleep, played games on the PlayStation 4 as if I were 15-years-old again, finally felt my eyes becoming as tired as I am of crying, awoke with tundra-like air stabbing my body and ran to the air conditioner to cut it off since I am trying to save money on my electricity bill this month, became cognizant that I am now meticulous about money since you left, ate a burger that I made sure was cooked well-done since you liked to eat your shit medium-well, listened to the music of younger rappers you introduced me to in an attempt to see if I would like them without you holding my hand and smiling at me, watched porn and cried because you seemed to be the only thing that could arouse me, typed some more of this poem at Starbucks, sent you a text message that told you that I missed you, waited two days for a response and didn't even have the privilege of having my message be left on read, made grits and eggs and sausage that I didn't even touch since I'm never hungry anymore, did at least 95 mph on highway 59 and didn't give a fuck about the cops, panicked like shit when my cop radar alerted me that 5-0 was indeed near, thanked God that another car was going as fast as me so I was able to slip away, regretted ever bringing you to my favorite restaurants, saw your face every single fucking time I saw the color red, stuffed the bracelet you gave me into the back of a drawer so that I would forget I have it, sat on the bathroom floor and cried when I went to retrieve it five seconds later, allowed it to sit in my hands and just exist which was nothing like I was doing, received a text message from you at 10:18 AM this morning as I folded three weeks' worth of clean-but-no-longer-smelling-like-laundry-detergent clothes, held my phone and wondered if a response was deserved, saw the value in myself and played sad music through my speakers, danced naked around my apartment and peered at a gorgeous human being that I met in the mirror, got dressed and went to lunch with people who care, ran four miles and didn't shed one tear, gave a homeless man the last seven dollars that I had to my name, chose to not do an ounce of homework since homework meant finding a home outside of you and remembering that I gave you a hoodie from my university as a gift, lifted weights in the gym and said, "Fuck you" every single time I completed a set, read a book of poetry by a black man who attends Harvard University and wondered if I would ever be that eloquent as you had took a chunk of me when you walked away—eloquence and dignity included, changed the password to my computer since it was your middle name, bought a salad from the place you and I had our first date, avariciously demolished said salad, smiled since I was taking back my life from you, went to the club and danced for two hours straight since you once told me that dancing was gay as fuck, felt great in my journey to becoming gay as fuck, ordered my usual Crown Apple and cranberry juice and didn't look back to see what you wanted to drink, missed you for a quick second but distracted myself with the music and laughter, took a shower that night and didn't think of you once, got dressed the next morning and looked in the mirror to see a fine ass nigga staring back at me, realized it was your loss, began to pour everything I had been pouring into you into the man who stood by my side as I fell in love with another man, asked him for forgiveness, held his hand as he fell asleep, stared at the ceiling and listened to him snore, held his hand a little tighter,

made it to day 12 of our break up alive, made the decision to take back the pieces of me that you took when you ended us, decided to leave this poem unfinished since every day I do something that helps me heal and grow and develop for myself,

decided on day 18 that I would resume writing this poem at 1:56 AM while drinking passion fruit tea and honey, felt the stinging defeat of rejection from a guy I met online and invited over to drink with me at my apartment, missed Jerome and wished I were in the United Kingdom with him so that he could focus on me and not work, contemplated the lyrics of several Frank Ocean songs, stared into a distance that seemed beyond my kitchen five feet away from me, obsessively sprayed the bath tub with cleaner and bleach and then scrubbed until my arms hurt, learned how to shave, nicked myself just above the left ear, thought about what it felt like to die from alcohol poisoning, determined it was too early in the morning for whisky, lazily picked up the novel I was to read for homework and flung it across the living room, walked the dogs at 2:56 AM and carried my knife for protection, smiled at the fact that I still cared enough about my own life to protect it, wished I were in bed holding you, wished I could kiss you, wished I could somehow change how our narrative was being written, regretted that you were the author, wished I could marry you, wished I could raise the gang of boisterous and vigorous boys we dreamed about, wished I could have met your mom more than once and impressed her enough that she advocated that you keep me around, wished I didn't see your naked body every time I close my eyes, wished I hadn't ever tasted you, cried two tears less than five, showered, slept, resolved to allow you to die in my mind and heart, vowed that I would never again be so foolish, stopped believing good people existed, tried screaming into a pillow, fell short of a yelp, cried and said your name aloud as I stared into a mirror, held the pillow like it was you since I wanted to give love and not hate, was ashamed at such a display of vulnerability,

took a deep breath with my eyes closed at 3:52 AM on day 25, still felt dead,

changed on day 26,

vowed to never give you anything of myself again yet still manage to offer you one tear when the thought of you is overwhelming (when is it ever not?) on day 54,

stared at the ceiling for most of the night on day 61,

texted you on day 62, felt the stinging rejection of your laughing emojis when I expressed to you that I still hurt, realized that you weren't shit, grew the fuck up and decided that I was too grown to play games with people who wanted to act like children, blocked your number, began a journey to loving myself—for real, for real this time, said "Fuck you" for the last time.

years after my graduation, at 10:20 AM

Now, my mother is a mother. She is complicated. And, I think she is now somewhat cognizant that she is bipolar. Or, at least, I'd like to think.

Society views her as a black woman living as a white woman because she is confused and lost and misguided.

I, however, view her as a black woman who is living as a black woman and always in search of white privilege that she thinks exists somewhere in the world as a tangible item that she can use.

She feels as though the Black Lives Matter movement is a fight that is to be fought. She trusts the police but does feel there is deeply ingrained corruption and injustice in America's justice system and society. She says that America's version of equality is a façade. She knows that her children can die any day because they are a part of what she once hated so fiercely. She prides herself on being biracial. She will always choose the "other" option when given an opportunity to define her race and then scoff at the idea that she was forced to choose anything. She is a firm believer in the second amendment. She is adamant that women are not appreciated enough by others in society and is quick to educate others on the struggles that women have had to face and still face today. And, she remains a ferocious detractor against the idea of her children eating watermelon and fried chicken.

an abandoning of morals

Seeing a black baby, her laugh so radiant and her skin so luminous, at the park while I run sends a memory into my lungs like a purple capsule filled with depression and grief. I stop running and sit. And think.

I remember my best friend being so quiet when I initially met her. I think it is why I gravitated toward her. She was always minding her business and was so invested in her own life and silence that I became invested in both of those, too. I assumed that she was glum and desired a friend. Yet, she would be the individual who would actually help me. Save me, even. At eighteen years old, we didn't realize how much of an adult she would have to be for the both of us.

The weekend was torturous for freshmen, especially since there was a campus ordinance dictating that we couldn't have cars. I was especially grateful for that since my mother had only enough money to send me to college with a care package that included new socks, underwear, and two weeks' worth of chicken-flavored Ramen noodles. I had read an article about the dangers of consuming too much of the noodles: cancer, high blood pressure. I decided to starve.

It was cheese. American cheese in a liquid-solid hybrid that came in a glass container and off-brand white tortilla chips. That's what Khadija offered to me when a group of us sat to talk and waste time—a collage of various shades of black. We were colors that didn't belong on a canvas. We were hues that could provoke, inspire, terrify.

I'm ravenous, I said to the group. A few of them, about four, laughed or chuckled. I wanted to establish myself as the funny guy. I preferred anything other than the gay guy.

We enjoyed some early evening conversations and cool breezes. It had been extremely hot that day and every single other day in the blistering, lonely openness of northern Louisiana.

Without an ounce of dignity or manners, I insatiably accepted the cheese and tortilla chips, cooled by her dorm room's refrigerator. She simply understood that I was hungry without me having to explain to her that I was a first-generation high school graduate and college freshman whose single-parent mother could not even afford to send me ten dollars in the mail. These were not words that she had to say. I just felt them emanate from her plus-sized being.

It was why, five years later, I understood that an abortion would help her keep her life on track. There was no explanation. No reasoning. Only understanding. We had defied the odds to enter our chosen careers immediately out of college and I wasn't going to allow her to become a statistic. When she asked for my advice, I didn't even have to think about it.

You are going to do it and then everything will be okay, I assured her.

You're sure, she asked.

Her voice was weak and muffled by tears that I knew plundered the slight curves of her brown eyes.

I'm sure, I said. I had lied to her for the first time in my life.

Okay. Thank you for answering the phone. I wish you were here right now. I need someone.

I wish I wasn't in fucking racist Arkansas dreading every single day I have to teach, I said. I wish I were there for you in this very moment, I continued. These kids make me miss college and our friends. Before we had to grow up. I chuckled, and I could feel her become more comfortable hearing me find humor.

I was making the mistake of only thinking about myself, instead of thinking about her and her life after this moment.

I pictured the faces of my tenth-grade students. I pictured how those faces would look when I surprised them with a pop quiz on the short story we'd read the day before.

Gaquez, I love you, she said. She was never this emotional. In fact, we were friends for about an entire year before she told me she loved me.

I love you, I said. She needed all of the love she could get in this moment. You, I resumed, are literally making me proud every day. I know that all of the nurses in Dallas probably hate you because you're so fucking intelligent. You'll be running your own hospital soon. I've told you that since I first met you.

I hoped her silence was indicative of her imagining it.

I'll call you when you it's done, she said more confidently.

I breathed a sigh of guilt when she hung up.

My friend, the woman who was unapologetically pro-life, was going to get an abortion in a couple of days. This was the girl who allowed me to use her cell phone our freshman year of college so that I could walk around pretending I owned one. She was the one who ordered pizza with her mother's credit card when I was experiencing freshman, sophomore, junior, and senior hunger pangs of college. This was the girl who was adamant that I sleep before making major decisions—I had always ignored her advice. And, now I told myself that I didn't know what to do when she needed me the most.

I should have hurriedly packed and driven to Dallas at that moment. Instead, I drank ginger ale and created tomorrow's pop quiz on Shirley Jackson's "The Lottery" for my tenth graders.

I immediately missed the days in which we could fuck up in a major way and it only meant failing a class for the semester.

an impeccable hurt

The third time was in a somewhat expensive Hampton Inn suite in Washington, D.C. on a brutal November night. We could hear the sounds of muffled, but familiar music coming from the streets. Snow fell, and I looked out of the seventh-floor window in awe. White could be so beautiful. I felt ashamed. Then angry...at myself.

Jerome's face was there in the crowd, one of the passersby. His caramel complexion, all six feet of him, his goofy laugh that could alleviate any of my pain, his smile, his striking brown eyes the shade of fresh leather. I knew he was in Louisiana patiently waiting for me to return to him after the conference. In a long-distance relationship, there were times in which he only wished to get a glance of my face on FaceTime. Maybe it was to remind himself that I was real, that what we had was real.

I'll keep you warm, he said to me as he held out his pale hands and thin arms. This white man's words to me were soft and lyrical. His arms were rather insignificant, yet I did feel protected by him when they were wrapped around my waist.

I peered down to the ground level, imagining the people walking were ants. Living in a city seemed so different from living in a rural area. Thinking of Arkansas made me feel nauseated. It reminded me of the harshness, the discomfort, the cruelty of white people. I never felt home there.

I don't need to be warm, I replied still looking out of the window searching for answers as to why I was in Washington, D.C. meeting up with my past and possibly ruining my future. I turned around to look at him sprawled across the lone, neatly-made bed. He knew that a messy bed annoyed me and had demanded that the hotel staff ensure the bed was *perfect*. White men, with their reservoirs of power shadowing behind them, could do stuff like that.

I made my way across the room anyway, tactfully surveying the décor that was especially unromantic and uninspiring. Is this what you think about when you're having an affair, I thought to myself. *Probably not. They are thinking about what horrible monsters they are. Am I a monster?*

It's hideous—the room, he said.

They should hire me to fix this place up, I said.

He could read my mind and see everything. That was a scary thought. I wondered if he had seen anyone's face when he was with me. Jerome appeared in my mind whenever Andy touched me or kissed me. He would smile and laugh, and the sound of it would shake me. His scent was so real, and I could smell Jerome's cologne on Andrew's neck.

He still sat on the bed, arms out, eager to be near me after so long. It was as though we needed a reminder of what *us* felt like. Nevertheless, we both could never forget the second time in Arkansas almost ten months prior: Andy had flown down from Boston to see me, spend some time, receive an answer to his one question.

In Arkansas, that lonely state, Andy had asked me to be with him. His face, perfectly defined and a little rugged with wispy, sandy-blond, and unusually long facial hair, was my mirror. His brown eyes weren't full of color that night. I sensed he yearned for a resounding yes.

I hadn't answered, or at least hadn't given him the answer he wanted. I promised to visit him soon in Boston when I grew weary of Arkansas.

I hadn't expected our next reunion to take place almost a year later.

That question wasn't important to me in this moment, in this hotel, but I could see it pirouetting inside of his head the entire night.

Now, there was no wine or takeout left, all of it avariciously consumed in celebration of our reunion. No balloons, no speeches, no toasts, only lovers. There was music. I heard the baritone of a muscle car. I didn't care much for cars, but I wanted to feel like a man with Andy.

    We talked about us. I kissed him between every couple of words or so. Marriage. *We could go to another state and leave the South for a liberal state.* Children. *I'll tell him I don't want children later.* Meeting each other's parents. *He will not meet my father.* No children. *Thank God.* Texas. *He would move to the South for me? There's no way I'm moving to Texas. Aren't there only cows there?*

    We lay on the sickening marsh green covers, staring into each other's eyes as if we both didn't have things to do in a few hours. I figured I could ignore the green and the large photographs of unappealing lobsters that lined the walls. I continued to look into his eyes, now alive after being seemingly revitalized by our embrace. They were brown; are brown. I realized I would never forget the color. Cheap milk chocolate that melted easily that had been decorated with gold sparks, similar to the ones that came out of a blow torch. I loved his eyes.

    I was supposed to wake in five hours. Sleep was not an option.

    Nothing mattered. It never did. Time stopped, or didn't, when I was with Andy.

    We laughed at jokes that were racially insensitive and discussed the plights of black teachers. That subject was less hilarious to me; he laughed and I did not.

    You take yourself too seriously, GQ, he said.

    Don't say that name, I told him.

    Alright, Gaquez, he whispered.

    I always wanted him to say my name the correct way. I craved intimacy with him in every possible manner. Hearing him say my name made me feel more real. There could be no other Gaquez in his life. I felt irreplaceable in the moments I was with him. In a way, I was already preparing for the end. I knew that my name would evoke *something* from him when we no longer spoke. That's exactly what I wanted. I wished to be remembered for eternity.

My lips slow-danced with his—off beat and ignorant of the music.

Do you love me, he said. He didn't ask.

Do you love me, I asked him.

You, first.

Andy, I do love you.

Then, leave him. Leave Arkansas and everything else. You could live with me and you could teach in Boston. You'd love it. I'd love it. Because I love you.

The drapes wavered and gossiped during our moment of silence as the air conditioner blew softly.

Andy, it doesn't work like that. I can't leave at the drop of a dime. I don't have money to come to Boston. I don't want to burden you. It would take me forever to find a job. And, what about Teach for America? Am I supposed to just drop out?

More wavering and gossiping from the drapes.

I knew that with every excuse I was breaking his heart. Could he handle the truth?

Could *I* handle the truth?

Lying on his chest, I could hear his heartbeat—panicked and irregular. Both of our bodies were sprawled over the unsightly green covers. The bed wasn't neat anymore.

He was lying there in silence. He bit his lip and blinked those lovely brown eyes aimlessly.

Andy, I said.

Yes, he said.

Two weeks.

Two weeks what?

All I need is two weeks and I'll come to Boston.

Two weeks and you'll come, he said as if our words were law. Again, he didn't ask. I assumed Harvard University had affected him so.

That's what I'm asking for, I said. I flipped my body over and looked into his eyes—those remarkable brown eyes.

Both of them able to look through with me a piercing lovingness, Jerome and Andrew were the same in some ways.

Ok, he said. He placed a kiss on my cheek. I could still feel his heartbeat, which was pounding rather hurriedly.

Ok, I agreed.

I want to hold you as you fall asleep since I don't know when I'll see you again, he said. His words weren't as soothing as they usually were.

Two weeks, I reminded him. *And two hours to sleep*, I reminded myself.

His arms held me and I attempted to feel at ease. His heartbeat wouldn't allow me to sleep. I could hear and feel its wailing through my back. It was hurt and blaming me for that hurt with every passing *bomp—bomp—bomp—bomp*.

We didn't care to turn off the hotel room's lights.

At 7 AM, my cell phone's alarm reminded me of the English teachers' conference I was expected at in an hour.

Andy tightened his grasp around my body. I didn't want him to let me go, but we both knew he had to.

I wriggled out of his hold and faced him. My face, so close to his, took every detail in.

His dirty blond hair, the unkempt barely-there mustache, eyes the color of newly-polished floorboards, short nose, small ears.

I didn't want to forget. My eyes were frantic. I couldn't forget.

We kissed a few times—short kisses that only meant that we care. We kissed two more times—long kisses that meant we love.

He decided to hug me one more time and pulled the covers off of me. He was allowing me to get out of bed while he was giving me the chance.

I crawled out of bed and slowly placed my left foot and then my right foot on the darker green carpet. I dressed quickly.

He stared at me. His face was solemn.

Andy, I said. Isn't this room so ugly? I looked around the space as I spoke.

Yes, he said. In any other moment, he would have laughed before responding.

It's our ugly room, I said.

He nodded and tears began to form in his eyes.

I rushed to him, placing my arms around his neck. I held him like that for five minutes. I didn't cry.

I'll check out at noon, he said.

Call me when your flight lands in Boston.

I will. Why did those words feel like he already knew that this was it?

I slowly removed my hands and stood up in front of him, I said trying to get more out of him conversation-wise; it was my attempt to figure him out.

Two weeks, I said.

See you, Gaquez. There was dread in his tone, a sense of fearfulness in letting me go. Or was it reprieve?

I walked away from the bed and quickly glanced back at him as I neared the room's door, the exit into the hallway and a life without him. He lay there smiling, and it hurt me because I knew he was holding back tears.

Two weeks, Andrew, I said softly as I exited the room. The door closed lightly.

On my taxi ride to the conference, as I hid my face from the driver, a cascade of tears fell.

to my mother, a black woman who didn't recognize she was black until she simply was

black woman fly fly fly to the sky, with your black beautiful self, with your amazingly empathetic but sometimes sanctimonious philosophies and attitude, with your class A cooking and ability to throw down in the kitchen for any man that you like, with your class A cooking and ability to throw down in the kitchen for any man that you love, with your class A cooking and ability to throw down in the kitchen for any man that you want the hell out of your house, with your ability to be the best cook and the worst host simultaneously when that man isn't treating you any good, with your black incredible self, with your flowing hair, with your kinky hair, with your hair that does what it wants to do and not what you want it to do, with your hair that smells like coconuts, with your hair that smells like lemon verbena, with your hair that smells like humidity that you could curse out since you just sat through what seemed like ten hours of micro-braiding, with your witty tongue, with your acerbic tongue, with your loving tongue, with your supportive tongue, with your knack for seeing the good in people when everyone else can't, with your knack for seeing how low-down and dirty a person truly is when everyone else can't, with your eyes that catch everything, with your ears that hear everything, with your sense to never admit that you saw it all so as to invite your colleague to provide you with more details even though you know all about it already, with your skin that is so delicate and kissed by God's lips, with your reservations about believing God is a he since women give life, with your newfound realization that God is a she since God gave life and you can give life so you both are equal, with your newfound realization that you may be God or at least a part of her, with your already-possessed realization that God is everything around you especially inside of you during your cycle when you are the most complex being that exists, with your notions about white women and other women who could never know how it feels like to be you, with your sadness when a man treats you wrong, with your sadness when a black man treats you wrong, with your sadness that men will always treat women wrong, with your resolve to ensure that your sons do not carry out that peculiar tradition of treating women wrong [who began that anyway?], with your lips, with your hips, with your hips that you had to learn to love since the world taught you they were unlovable, with your mind, with your intelligent and too-quick-for-dim-people mind, with your breasts and the nutrients within them, with your breasts that five children drank from, with your breasts that this nation of Amerika-ka-ka was/is nourished by, with your laugh, with your laugh that is unapologetically unique and raucous and quiet and reserved all together since one word cannot properly describe anything that you are, with your black beautiful self.

old dominion, on the steps of the wet concrete stairs

I sat on the stairs, somewhat drunk, somewhat reprehensible, somewhat pitiful. The red Moscato I slowly drank, bitter and acidic, soothed my throat. Within it was angst, deservedly mine but unwarranted.

It was the summer, but I didn't care much that I was sweating. It almost seemed therapeutic.

I had run earlier. It was during my run that I realized that we needed to speak. That I needed to see his face. I ran to clear my mind, but his laugh wouldn't dissipate from my conscience even as I turned the volume up and invited the raucous music into my body.

The concrete hurt me as I rubbed against it with my bare legs, but my heart did too, so I stuck with the tradition of pain and remained there. On the concrete stairs, not going up, not getting higher, not making any progress.

The sleepy, monotonous, gray apartment complex was rather large and was constructed like a maze. Its puzzling nature spoke to me. Residents seemed lost as they entered and headed to their individual brick apartments. Was it comical—to watch them scurry and search as if they were ants? I supposed it wasn't fair for anyone to have to search for a home, for something that feels like home; it's supposed to feel natural; be easily accessible. It wasn't fair to watch them appear lost.

I was lost, too.

That's why I was calling him.

Perhaps.

His name and picture shone on the screen on my iPhone 6s, and for a second, I wished it was an archaic flip phone. No faces, no FaceTime, no awkwardness in seeing his face for the first time in a year and a half.

He was leaving my house in a state of bliss. It was the second time. He had flown in from Boston to visit me during a deplorable Arkansan January.

It reminded me of the first time, in Mississippi, when I had placed my life on hold and devoured every significant and trivial fact about him. A black man whose pride in his blackness and newfound resentment against whiteness was a stark contrast to a white man who was cognizant of his white privilege and empathized with blackness yet did not cower when approached by *my* blackness. It was his awareness that caused me to fall in love with him. That and all of the nights we spent sitting in my dark green 1999 Honda Accord talking about life and the mosquitoes that stalked us. I was in love with a white man— Though, I was also in love with another man who knew nothing about Andrew.

Andy, call me as soon as you land in Boston, ok?

That's what I said to Andrew as he solemnly walked away after holding me for a few minutes in an embrace that signified impending doom. I ran to him not wanting him to leave without feeling my touch again, aware that this would probably be the end. I hadn't made a decision and it had hurt him. We both knew it, yet I kissed him again as if he was the only man in my life.

I only drank wine with him then. It had once been our way of celebrating our time together—those lonely events in which he and I studied each other with the astuteness of students who either passed the exam or died in their efforts. He was that serious for me—a white man who had allowed me to love him in the unapologetically black way that I could.

On those stairs of concrete in Texas, I sat wondering whether or not he was going to answer the call. A call for help. *My* call to him.

My third glass of wine was halfway gone. I drank wine to remember him now. It was my way of coming to terms with his absence.

He liked my independence. And, I was showing none. I choked on a large gulp of wine and low self-esteem.

What's up, he said when he answered.

Light brown, bushy eyebrows. Dirty, blond hair. I consumed every detail in an effort to make up for lost time and forgotten features. It hurt me to forget how his nose curved or how small his face was or how crooked his smile was. His crooked smile begged for my attention. I smiled, too. I felt glad to see he was still himself.

Andy, I just—I began.

Don't spoil it, he said.

I miss—I resumed.

Again, don't spoil it, he said with more force than before.

We talked about the unforgiving Boston snow and the dreadful Houston traffic. And, then he said he was glad I was willing to still be his friend.

Andy, I can't be your friend. I've told you that, I said. His silence was indicative of what had grown between us—a scathing disconnection that no amount of running could fix.

He silently watched as I drank the bit of the wine that was left.

I don't drink anymore, he said.

I wondered if it was because of me.

We talked about the experiences of his Harvard and my University of St. Thomas.

I don't think we talked about us. I wanted to. But, he wanted to remain friends.

I really care about you, Gaquez, he said. His words were sincere. I felt them, but I ignored them.

Do you, Andy, I asked him. I think that question hurt him. The concrete hurt me. I figured we were equal.

I gotta go, ok?

His words viciously stung me. There was a time a wasp had stung me—it had flown into the opening of my shirt underneath my right shoulder and landed on my body. I had panicked and flounced everywhere in an attempt to evade the touch of an unwelcome visitor. I felt a tiny prick of fire in my skin covering the right side of my ribs. It was a cigarette extinguished on my skin and left there to fizzle out. I yelled—half of me surprised that it had actually stung me and half of me in pain. But Andy's sting was 100 times worse. It was pain that I couldn't fix with peroxide or alcohol. He had this silent, deadly ability to crush my heart with apathy and a lack of empathy. It was not the Andy I had once fallen in love with.

    I do, too, I said.

    I craved more wine, more numbness.

    I ran again later that night.

rush hour traffic—lonely rush hour traffic

  I think about these people in my dreams. My daydreams. Vivid, lucid, yet not distracting as I focus on the miles-long line of cars in front me. I see them: the woman with short auburn hair who seemingly stares with eyes that are empty; a man who smiles and laughs as he listens to rap music I have not heard yet; a grandfather who may be drunk or have haphazard vision.
  I'm on the other side of this Houston highway traveling south. They're traveling north, but I can't seem to wonder if they are moving in the same direction as me. Are they expecting a promotion, anticipating a marriage proposal from their partner, have they been cheated on? It aches me to not know their stories, to have no context for their lives. Mostly, I seem to not have any for my own.
  What about their lives? I wonder if they, too, have had to sit and listen to the ramblings of a teenager who has never learned how to properly announce himself as the gay son of the family.
  He said, you aren't supposed to be this way.
  He said, it's my fault that you want to be a woman.
  He said, only a weak man would choose to be like…feel like a woman.
  There is no brash or brazen response to his words. I don't feel like myself after his words stab me mercilessly. My body does not move, my mouth cannot articulate, my brain will not comprehend.
  But, that was six years ago. And, this is now.
  This is Houston, and in this city, we play a game of stop-and-go-driving—mostly during early mornings and early evenings. I don't think anyone wins the game, but no one wants to lose and wait for Mike's (or one of his many cousins') towing services.
  So, I dodge and dart around this car and that car as I think about what I want people to think when they see me.

I think for a while. My head hurts, but I continue to think.

I acquiesce to defeat. I don't care. I say it again louder to myself. I press the power button on my radio and scream it aloud. The driver of the Nissan Altima next to me looks over at me with concerned eyes. I smile.

She thinks I'm crazy, I think. You are crazy, my conscience agrees. This isn't about me, I tell myself. Yet, it is. This awareness comes from a voice I cannot pinpoint.

I change lanes and feel relief. I have won today's game. Other winners, seemingly joyous, cruise along me as I accelerate to almost 85 MPH. This is what I want. This is what I need. Freedom.

I peer out of my driver's side window, wondering what the drivers on the other side of the highway think of me and my recklessness.

WHITE this and WHITE that

"Shut up," she utters coldly. The words ooze malice and pollute my clean classroom.

The classroom, I think, as I rectify my mistake of claiming ownership of anything in the desolate town of El Dorado, Arkansas, its candy shops and pizzerias included. The classroom, even with 30 young and lively bodies in it, including my own, is not home and will never be home because I am not what normally calls this place home. Carpet usually muffles sounds, but the drab, old gray carpet here doesn't muffle anything except my footsteps as I pace around the large space. Its walls, white as chalk, serve as a reminder that I am not white and never will be. There is much that will never be in El Dorado High School.

"Hannah, I…"

"Shut up!"

"I fully affirm your feelings. However, you have to make the decision to compose yourself and handle your anger in ways that don't include lashing out at people."

"You keep talking about white this and white that. I'm tired of it."

"Well, that's because America is all about white this and white that. There's hardly enough room for anyone else."

"You say we have white privilege," she begins as her hand wavers in an attempt to include her classmates in a war being waged against me, "but I still don't see it."

"And, you won't, Hannah."

"See? You call me blind and dumb without telling me what I'm not seeing."

"I…look, you will not see your privilege because you benefit from it. You are accustomed to it. It is in you, readily accessible at all opportune moments in your life. I'm not saying that you will not struggle. I am not stating that you will live a life free of conflict and pain and sadness and despair and love and happiness and anticipation. Furthermore, I never directly said you are blind. I am only inferring that you are blind. Your refusal to recognize your blindness is evidence of your privilege. See?"

"Dumb nigger."

"What in the hell did you call me?"

"I warned you to stop talking about me."

"I am talking about the blindness of white people, not you. Get out of my classroom." Damn. It is *my* classroom again.

"Gladly."

"I'm waiting…"

"Can I get my things?"

"Hannah, you may leave at this moment."

"I hate this class and I hate you."

"Thank you, Hannah."

"Thank *you*, Mr. Jackson." Her sarcasm is a warm reminder that I have a few weeks before I quit teaching—black men cannot teach in El Dorado, Arkansas.

in the delta

Cleveland, Mississippi was the loneliest city I had ever visited. Hordes of mosquitoes clung to my arms and legs, relishing in my perspiration without a regard for the life they sucked from me or the hundreds of other recent college grads housed in a new dormitory building on Delta State University's campus.

We were there to become teachers, newly accepted members into a famous organization known as Teach for America. However, that didn't stop the people of Mississippi or Arkansas, where I later taught, from naming us, people of Teach America. It was rather bothersome but when you are young, and you care about your role in life, it can be annoying to feel as though people neglect you so much that they don't care to name you or classify you correctly. It's the same thing as being called by another name when you know damn well your mother (or father) named you something else.

Hell no. You tell them that your name is Gaquez. Juh-quez, just like I pronounce it. All you have in this damn world is your name. Don't let people fuck it up, my mother had once yelled at me as I ran out of the door and on to school to escape the madness of my childhood, or the lack thereof.

When I introduced myself to Andrew, he had pronounced it Gah-quez. His eyes, I remember those damn brown eyes—gorgeous and distracting, I couldn't focus on correcting him. She—my mother—was screaming at me inside of my head.

Gaquez, I said to him, motioning with my hands that I wanted him to repeat after me.

Gaquez, he said lightly. There was understanding in his tone. I knew he cared about me the first time he spoke my name correctly.

I had walked up to him, out of the blue. I didn't know what to say or do except say what I wanted. I asked him if he wanted to have lunch or dinner?

Are you asking me out on a date, he asked?

Yes, I said.

You're very forward, he said and chuckled.

Just tell me where.

Hmmmm…let's do Mexican.

I secretly harbored disdain for Mexican food. It never seemed to agree with my stomach. But, I agreed. Am I picking you up, or…?

Yes, you'll be picking me up. I don't have a car, he said.

How old are you?

He seemed to realize where I was going with our conversation. Well, I am 27 years old and I don't have a car because most people in Boston don't have a car. Our city has an extensive public transportation system.

He is from the North, I thought. I want to know more about where you come from and all of that. I've never been more northern than Kentucky, I said.

His eyes widened. Cool, he said.

We shook hands and parted ways—his way was to a staff meeting as he was employed by Teach for America as a model teacher and my way was to the late-night printing station so that I could take care of the copies I needed for my practice students the next day.

It was almost midnight. I couldn't sleep—the excitement about going on a date with a white man was enough to keep me awake.

a necessary loss of cohesion

Is this what depression feels like? Is this what it feels like to want to actually murder yourself? I've felt an ounce of this before, but never like this. I could die.

I grasp the steering wheel, allowing tears to escape from my eyes. I pull over and listen to the '90s R&B loudly playing from my radio. Not even the raucousness can block out this burden of a feeling. Heaviness. It hurts.

I cry. For what? I don't know.

At 7 AM on a rude Monday, he called me to tell me that he wanted me to see her. We hadn't talked in so long, almost two years. I couldn't remember exactly what his face looked like. And he had gotten braces and had them removed, so his smile wasn't familiar. My brother reneged on his promise to keep his daughter in my life, to keep himself in my life. We have not spoken in years.

I don't think I've ever felt a pain like the one that struck my body as he told me that I tested positive. Two lines, that's how I learned to make a positive sign in elementary school. We were learning addition and I was a natural. 2+2=4. Easy. There was a boy who cried because he couldn't add as quickly as the rest of us. He wore navy blue pants with a hunter green polo shirt. That was the year they made us begin wearing uniforms. Louisiana was always backwards like that. No individuality. Just becoming content with achieving nothing more in life than a body riddled with mosquito bites. I was not that person.

I felt like a failure the first time I felt a needle penetrate the muscle of my buttocks. This is what it feels like to have an STD for the first time. Silver, cold silver, the silver that you don't want to touch, the silver that is used to make bullets for use against mythical werewolves, that was the silver that was being injected into me and racing through my veins. She said it was penicillin. But, how could medicine feel so evil?

It is my anger at generational wealth that I find myself obsessed with. I listen intently as my Literary Criticism professor pronounces words in a supercilious manner that tells me that I will never be her. I think about how my application to Rice University has been denied two years in a row, and how she brags about her effortless experience there as if people like me don't exist.

I want all of my tears back, I said. There was intense seriousness in my tone. I was owed—fate was indebted to me. I slashed at the sea with hands that mimicked wicked blades, silver cutting and slicing. The Gulf of Mexico's waters reciprocated every hack with a splash that sprayed my face, neck, and chest with its blood.

How could I arrive an hour late to the interview that could change my trajectory? I sit in the museum, abashedly, and painfully silent. Who makes such a careless mistake? I am sure I will not get the job, even when I am allowed to walk into the room and dazzle the interviewers with my shine. Being black and being not perfect are not acceptable in corporate America. I'll probably have the black-people-are-always-late jokes made behind my back once the interview is over. They'll probably mimic my apology. I sit and think about how I can turn this around, how my charm can turn my apology into a winner. My charm is wearing off. I just turned 26-years-old. I'm not the young, energetic man I once was 8 days ago. I have entered my second quarter of a century—there is no excuse as to why I am not a proud owner of a home with a white picket fence. All of that jazz and bullshit. Why do we strive to meet standards that are seemingly impossible—actually impossible?

I don't understand how age doesn't guarantee stability. That dream was sold to me, and I bought it, invested in it, and

expected dividends. Now, I am broke and broken.
There are people on the streets with PhDs who are homeless and unemployed. Will I be one of them?

None of this makes fucking sense.

Three/fifths

I.
My text message to her this afternoon was meant to be a reparation of sorts for the shit we'd put her through during our childhood. She was the middle child and, subsequently the most ignored and least loved. She was our mother's first daughter and her worst enemy. There was nothing the rest of us could do in alleviating the tension that existed for years between our mother and sister. Unfortunately, we made it worse. The text read:

~~Enistazha, I'm so sorry for everything. I don't know what we were doing when we were younger. We were just young and dumb, right? I apologize for all of the hurtful things that I said to you out of anger when I felt as if that was the only way to hurt you. It was not fair. We had a hard life. No one had shown us how to properly love another person. Look at our mother. Look at our uncles and aunts, who so quickly turn against each other in times of misunderstanding and miscommunication.~~

[my finger obsessively pressed the backspace button]

~~Enistazha, life wasn't always easy for us. Life definitely wasn't easy for you. I apologize for being such an asshole when we were younger and even now as we are adults. I've always assumed that since we didn't have a father in our lives, I had to be that father to my siblings. Only recently have I realized that I didn't need to be a father so early in my life. I wanted to be a father so that I could feel as though I could influence and control and oversee. I was a horrible father—angry, impulsive, insecure, manipulative, naïve, disrespectful, power-hungry, controlling, uncompassionate, harsh. I apologize for attempting to be the parent that I thought our mother should have been. I apologize for every single time I called you fat or referred to you as a bitch.~~

[my finger obsessively pressed the backspace button]

~~An adage that I've grown to understand and apply to my life is this one: Hurt people hurt people. It is so true. I find myself wondering how much heartache and sorrow I could have avoided by simply knowing and viewing life through the eyes of someone who understood such profound words. For this, this exploration of my feelings through a selfish perspective during an apology to you, I apologize. It has been so easy for me to think about myself and my ideas, aspirations, opinions. Instead, I should have given time to you and our siblings to try and understand what exactly it was to understand about you all. I've failed in this regard, but I do want to ensure that I am the most supportive and loving brother that I could possibly be from this point on. Shouldn't we be able to support each other mentally and emotionally? It's a significant job for those of us who are significant enough to be siblings to others. Lastly, I apologize for not telling you three words that could have made so much of a difference in your life when you needed them the most.~~

[my finger obsessively pressed the backspace button]

I love you, Nay.

DL

I don't speak French, he says. Who is this "we" you speak of, he asks. I have not grown an inch since I was eighteen years old. And, yet, in that instant, I grew silent.

we want green

green is killing our babies, uprooting the folks who have planted trees in their homes hoping that the new buds and blossoms will be promising, hurting those who want the best for these new saplings that once would have become great oaks and maples and pines, allowing for the ignorance of these new babies to fester like sores that have been neglected by the doctors who have all of the necessary tools to treat them, granting these new babies the domain to carry out long-protected traditions and customs in manners that are unfitting for the royalty they do not realize they are, cutting us off from the ancestors who so desperately cry out to us in order to tell us that we must cry out to them for they know everything that will happen after we are gone from this place, intruding upon the innocence we as a people once so graciously respected, green is killing our babies, killing us one by one on the streets so that others can make a profit off of it, killing us one by one in the schools so that others can make a profit off of it, killing us one by one in the jails so that others can make a profit off of it, killing one by one in our neighborhoods so that others can make a profit off of it, killing us slowly, and painfully, and revengefully, and hatefully, and with malice, green is killing our babies who think they are adults who can make adult decisions who are then damaged by the consequences of those decisions, who look into the eyes of a child who is looking for a child to be its mother/father, who doesn't know the implications of being black and young in this country, who looks to a future only five minutes from now and not longer than that since social media has fostered an attitude of impatience and self-gratification, who needs our help, who is begging for our help, who requires our help through a little kind interaction and some words and some laughs and some tears and some time to combat the trauma they have experienced as a new sapling in this world that expects everyone to be redwoods.

gay bar

My friend's sandals were less like the shoes of Jesus and more like an embellished mosaic, each of them embedded with turquoise and orange beads whose hues were neither loud nor subdued. They were solemnly intriguing. It was to be expected that he wore something that screamed cultural appropriation. In my experience, I'd deduced that this was not in an ignorant or malicious manner. He appreciated the world; he relished in being able to convey this through his attire. His face always gave off a florid aura, as if somehow blood could not be in any other part of his body. He smiled his seemingly contrived smile and leaned in to hug me when he got into my rental car. Though, Ken was anything but contrived. His movements were natural; he was a free spirit inspired to move as if his world were three-dimensional as it was for the birds and fish.

The drive to the coffee shop we had first solidified our friendship at several months prior wasn't significant. In the midst of odd light Houston traffic, we discussed what we perceived to be disloyalty from those we trusted the most. And, we talked about how we had to become cognizant of life and its intricacies. My foot shifted from accelerator to brake frequently as we approached red light after red light. And, our conversation continued in a monotonous manner that didn't quite match the way in which our tones highlighted certain injustices in our friendships.

I held the door for him to enter into the coffee shop as I wanted to be the last to walk in. It was mostly because I needed an opportunity to scope out the room inconspicuously before becoming an awkward foreigner. I mean to say, coffee drinkers are acutely aware so feeling a space and trying to feel safe in it is important for me. The bar was safe, and we talked. Words were lost and found as we laughed and attempted to heal each other's wounds. This was life, and life wasn't fair. I drank an entire caramel latte with soy milk in about five minutes. He could tell I was nervous about something and pushed me to reveal this concealed turmoil. I withdrew—he was patient. We left as if we had been restored by the shop's atmosphere, and he asked if I wanted to go somewhere else before the mayor-issued curfew took effect.

    He was fascinating the first day I ever met him. Dominick, as he introduced himself, was stoic in an avant-garde and pretentious way. This pretentiousness was harmless. He seemed to be the most poisonous flower in the room at the time but turned out to be the gentlest sunflower you could ever allow your fingers to touch. His aura was in a constant state of contradiction, and I felt myself compelled to it. I wanted to know how he was able to endure the pain of a sun swallowed; how light could shine and enlighten one's spirit yet cause such exhaustion and melancholy. He could be a deity if he wished—there was a necessity for his presence. It was as if he represented what everyone was feeling and who they were exactly. He carried himself with the swagger of a popular politician with integrity and the aloofness of a strict Catholic librarian. It was this indifference that gave him god-like ascriptions. No one would have believed in him, though. Ken wouldn't want them to. He was a giver, and gods were takers, receivers, beneficiaries who gave only pebbles of hope to those invested in buying such trinkets.

    We did not begin as friends, but he was my friend.

    Dominick died as our relationship strengthened and I simply knew Ken.

    I look at him now as we sit at one of Houston's most popular gay bars, his attention on the dark sky marred by devastation and curses thrown out at it by an entire city. We were drinking to forget how Hurricane Harvey had just changed the courses of hundreds of thousands of lives, including our own. This was life, and life wasn't fair. Our conversation was of silence, no more characterized by the catachresis it usually is. What adjectives, verbs, and nouns we utilized in the gaps between moments of silence are insignificant. Our language was one even we didn't understand. And though I sometimes struggled to comprehend what he was saying in that language, I knew that he was speaking through love. This is what he wanted to give to the world. This is what was fair to him. He would make a horrible god.

Would you eat your grandchild with a fork and knife or on the way to work if you hadn't had the chance to cook breakfast?

A quick reminder to the white women in my American Girl in Literature class who have biracial grandchildren and thought it appropriate to display a lack of couth when speaking on how they were created:

DO NOT trivialize the enigma of a black woman. DO NOT diminish her black babies into flavors. DO NOT metaphorically devour her blackness. DO NOT salivate when you see her shine, shimmer, and sparkle. She is glistening night fall with skin holding all of it together like the glue that held together generations of African peoples before and after they were enslaved. She is bright sunrise with shades of yellow, orange, red, and purple. She is the afternoon sky, bright as the sun's rays which are brighter than itself.

A diminished shine;

        You passed me up sister
We were in the supermarket and you passed me up
I gave you a smile
A little smile
A nod of my head and i managed to do it all so gracefully in attempt to mirror your elegance when i noticed you
I was reminded of my mother and i missed her
She's in west Virginia
So i had it on my heart to say hello and give you a smile but you were too busy worrying about your day's troubles and if your melanin was fashionable as it dripped in gold that was much duller than yourself.
        You passed me up brother
I managed to offer a friendly smile when we briefly made eye contact on aisle 5
The bread and crackers
But you didn't smile back because black men don't smile
That's gay
Smiling and exulting in the beauty of being happy is gay
I walked away feeling as though this lesson had been instilled in me already
I was the student yet again to a concept i wished would cease to have significant meaning in my existence as did Avogadro's number and the Pythagorean theorem from middle school
Black men don't allow me to be a man.
        We were in the checkout line together so courtesy begged you to say hello to me brother and i replied without any energy
Softly
My confidence and glimmer diminished by my last two interactions with people who look like me
So my hello was weak
Mild-mannered
Feeble

i could tell you were tired too
Tired of life's days and nights but seeking
Almost begging
For the shine of others for energy to continue on
But
i don't know what vitality looks like this morning
You even try again and ask me
How are you
you smile as you say the words
i don't return the smile because
i assume it is forced
And your sincerity is wasted on a young man who looks like you.
    i passed you up brother.
    This is what it feels like to be black on a rainy Monday morning.

To be black in Cuba is to be beautiful in Cuba, because no one knows or cares that I am gay.

They recognize me now that I have been here for three days; the Cubanos still look at me as if I am different, though. It is loud in Cuba, not in a jarring Mexico City way but in a I'm-annoyed-that-wonderfully-expensive-hellos-and-good mornings-in-Spanish-from-poor-beautiful-people-have-woken-me-from-sleep-that-was-already-difficult-to-get way.

The mosquitoes aren't up this early as the sunrise has forced them to hibernate. There is a rooster around the corner that crows almost as raucously as the Cubanos move throughout Havana.

I've grown accustomed to not being able to breathe—I admit this is a difficult reality to accept as a man who has thrived in the forests of Louisiana all of his life. It's both the violent exhausts of Cuba's ancient automobiles and a stifling combination of heat and humidity that I've never experienced before.

Guilt plagues me. My thoughts are somewhat sinful, for who needs Africa when there is blackness in every hue in every direction that my eyes can move. An interesting debate of whether sight, taste, or touch happens to be God's greatest creation occurs in my head. What was God, as I imagine her as every being in the universe and defined by effervescence and shine, intending? Can she see beauty even in the ugliest of us? Can she see beauty in me? I am beautiful now, on my 26th birthday, but what will I be tomorrow when I awake?

I scream to the metaphorical mountain tops of Houston, Texas

Reminder to myself:

Remember
ANGELA DAVIS,
ASSATA SHAKUR,
BARBARA JORDAN,
IDA B. WELLS,
HARRIET TUBMAN,
FANNIE LOU HAMER,
FRED HAMPTON,
HUEY NEWTON,
STOKELY CARMICHAEL,
MALCOLM X,
NAT TURNER,
BOBBY SEALE,
MARCUS GARVEY,
and so many
others.

Remember
their lives
and narratives.

Remember
Black History.

As I stand in the water that reminds me of my mother's womb; a familiarity with God

Mexico, you're my everything.

7-feet-tall at 10:58 PM; the first time I ever fell in love

Lacking the innate ability required to console, I fumble the ball and lose the game. Yet, you are comforted by my palm on your thigh. I can't remember ever having possessed the ability to help someone understand me, and that is a fatal flaw in this moment.

My Nissan Sentra is not spacious enough for a man who is seven feet tall, but you tell me that you're comfortable. Why you have always attempted to comfort me by denying your comfort baffles me.

And now, in this moment, you subtly shake with nervousness. It has been only the second time you've seen me in five years. I place my palm on your lap, an action that has a calming effect.

Is this normal? Is this what former lovers do? Meet up and attempt to reconcile? Attempt to mutually recompense the other for time lost, damage accumulated, pain harvested.

I once heard one of my late professors say that pain is more easily grown and harvested than corn while I was a college freshman. At that moment, that quote seemed reductive and useless. Seven years later, I know what he meant.

At Waffle House, you entreat me to utilize what heart you assume I have left.

I cannot oblige, and I eat my waffle, scrambled eggs, and grits without so much as an ounce of regret in my denial to love you again.

How the tables have turned—you once taught me that love is something that floats centimeters above your welcoming palm, that love nearly touches your skin, that love is fleeting, that love is a phenomenon best enjoyed drunk, that love pushes you to the brink of becoming psychotic, that love, itself, is psychotic, that love is a practice more foolish than religion, that it is indeed blinding, that love is a resolve to become engage in the folly of a kamikaze.

You are the only seven-feet-tall man I've ever made cry. I loved you once, but now your tears are not welcome guests.

I cannot even promise that in another life I would be the selfless man that you love to conceptualize in place of the ambition and selfishness that I embody in this moment in my life.

With you, I only speak of 'you's' and 'I's'; even subconsciously there are no 'we's'. Too much weight—I don't employ the resolve to lift it.

Yet, even then you ignore how I proactively reveal to you that what we had is in the past.

At the park, with the romantic gestures of nature with her bright green grass and soothing zephyrs, you fail to truly understand that we no longer have that spark. This is the electricity that is required between human beings if they wish to love each other sincerely.

Using your skin to write my story; to speak your story

Hideous, definitive smirks impair my ability to chuckle lightly and see the humor in his jokes when he mentions his height. 5 feet and eleven inches. *Though I know he's an inch shorter than that.* Disillusioned by the LGBTQIA community, *much like myself. We both have some deep-rooted insecurities and hang-ups with masculinity.* Materialistic. Not excited about the way in which the world is out there to explore, mostly because he is only able to view his surroundings within a five-feet radius. There are moments at which he displays the tenacity of a 26-year-old *who has been empowered by an old episode of Oprah or some sob story that concludes with the ultimate achievement of success*, when he can connect and prove that his age is not a disability. This is when he gleams, glistens, glosses. This is when he is magnificent. A fresh newspaper. One that has never been touched—that is what he reminds me of as my fingers run through his curly black hair and across his vanilla scone-baked skin. Braille is upon him, and I access the knowledge imprinted into the pores of his epidermis.

    He is gone.

Black women taught me how to read books; a black, gay man taught me how to read myself

Navigating through life in a constant state of rage is something James Baldwin warned me about. He's a fucking genius [*I would hope he would smile at this compliment and offer me a cup of coffee and intimate conversation, while also coolly revealing to me that Maya Angelou would be joining us*]; his euphemisms and cackle exist in my mind. We could have been friends; black and gay and men and writers. He *is* a writer and I, at least, *pretend* to be one. But, definitively, he is a writer. And it is Wednesday, so I don't know what the hell I am at the moment. Where are you, James? [*My professor once remarked that an English student should never address a writer by first name unless we intimately knew them*]. Why am I surrounded by a sea of black and gay and malice? There is no you in this crowd, and I flail to stay afloat without having to drown the people in my proximity. But, how else can I rise above the waves? I do not want to be like these men. I am not willing to obliterate the building blocks of another's life to feel a temporary triumph of becoming a conquistador. It's rather fucking annoying. [*I would curse every other word or so in order to get my point across. There is a liberation in profanity. Though, I doubt Maya Angelou would smile at my display of such lewdness in the company of others*].

For John, my former supervisor, who has been taught that dominance is intimidation [written before he became one of my closest friends in life]

establishing dominance

does not mean ensuring the room is quiet.
It does not mean standing when everyone else is sitting.
It does not mean having the last word.
It does not mean asserting who are as the transcendental signified.
It does not mean monopolizing a discussion.
It does not mean announcing that you are the leader as the room watches.
It does not mean interpreting for those quite capable of interpreting for themselves.
It does not mean becoming a father.
It does not mean having high expectations and becoming disappointed in me when I refuse to adhere to those expectations.
It does not mean threatening others in a passive-aggressive manner.
It does not mean bringing your baggage into your professional life.
It does not mean that your voice must be heard.
It does not mean speaking for others.
It does not means refusing to pass the microphone.
It does not mean becoming the teacher in any relationship.
It does not mean not taking into consideration how others view themselves.

this is not how establishing dominance is defined.

Galveston beach; one of them

We talk about white people's generational wealth but neglect to consider black people's generational habits. This is the topic of discussion while Jerome and I drive to Grambling, Louisiana.

The location of Grambling State University is a home not forgotten—it is where we met and where I became a man.

Shreveport, Louisiana looms behind us, his grandmother's funeral having taken all of our morning and every bit of emotional energy we were conserving for events that usually require all of it.

I type as he drives. Guilt slashes at my conscience. My fingers spring to action, and I begin writing this very piece.

This man is amazing. Jerome, I mean. He was everything I could have asked for four and a half years ago when we met.

Even then he was the embodiment of a simultaneous aloofness and allure. At the first party we ever ran into each other before falling in love, he intentionally danced with every other person and chose to ignore me. Pressed to know why exactly how he could ignore me, I relentlessly pursued a friendship. This, too, was ignored.

Now, he is keenly focused on the road and I decide knowing why he never danced with me at the party is something that I can live without.

At that same party five years prior, I had lost some trivial item. Jerome had found it and brought it to me. I had cooked dinner and invited him in on a whim. He said he could stay for 15 minutes and kept me company for more than four hours. We saw each other every single day after that evening.

I watch him, and I realize that he is exactly what my life has needed for so long: a calmness that is impossible to believe exists. With a palm, a kiss, a word, he can provide clarity and quiet to my world.

I don't know how to do that for him in this moment when

he has lost a woman he loves.

México, ¿quién soy yo?

Mexico City, you are my everything. This is the thought I think before taking the first shot of authentic tequila—a hearty raucous Mexican chuckle helps to cut the sharpness of the liquor.

"Don Julio! Las cosas reales, the real stuff," our Airbnb host declares. He is my complexion, a hue of snicker doodle cookie left in the oven a few minutes too long. He—Oscar—speaks and moves about with an American confidence. I feel ashamed at this observation. Perhaps I am moving and speaking with a newfound Mexican confidence.

I feel relieved to have corrected myself. America isn't so great—it's why I came to Mexico for a weekend.

Our host explains that Don Julio tequila is expensive.

Its taste is dry and sharp, much like the air of the city. One can breathe, but it is almost as if one has to labor to inhale and exhale. It is peaceful, though.

I later found out that Mexico City is one of the world's most polluted cities.

"Muchas gracias por este señor," I clumsily state in lousy Spanish. I imagine this tequila—a man's man tequila, Ernest Hemingway's type of tequila—is getting to me already. My traveling companion, Jerome, nods in solidarity. It is a kind way to welcome us to the country.

We are in an area of the city called the Zocalo.

The balcony of the condo allows me to see the entire city, La Ciudad de México, and everything it offers. Don Julio makes me feel high, like I feel when I look down at the people on the streets of the city.

Even on the 22nd floor, I hear the music—it is an incessant orchestra of chaos. There are not many ways it can be described. I smell the food; spices, chicken, beef, vegetables, myriad types of bread.

My descriptions are reductive—they do it no justice. I am experiencing the country's dia de los Muertos, Day of the Dead.

"We do this for them." My host struggles with English as much as I do Spanish. This is comforting. He explains what the holiday means to Mexicans and those who celebrate it. He warns us that we will not get sleep. 22 floors up from the street will not help to silence the celebration of so many people living and teaching that death is not to be feared.

"That is admirable," Jerome remarks.

Our host smiles. I don't think he understands what admirable means.

It is the tequila that all three of us do understand. We take another shot in unison.

A short flight from Houston, Texas to Mexico City's Benito Juárez International Airport has only fueled the curiosity we have to explore. Our home host gives us some directions in Spanish [we are much better at understanding and interpreting than speaking] and we leave the condo.

The elevator rides down to the lobby of the condominium are the only peaceful moments during my trip. I close my eyes and allow it to swallow my insecurities and preconceptions. I need to be empty and willing to learn while in Mexico City.

I need to be able to drink. This is how I explore the world around me—in awe and not-so-reprehensibly-but-almost drunk.

We walk into the glaring sun and onto the street, Paseo de la Reforma 27, blending in with the crowd—Mexico allows you to do that. It is familiar, maternal, soothing. This is simultaneous with the parade's boisterousness. I march in tandem with my hosts, all of them welcoming me with camaraderie and laughter.

Jerome and I visit a bar after marching for about one hour and into a section of the city that is so different from where we will be staying, one that doesn't look normal.

It is dark inside, and we welcome the unexpected. Patrons sit and drink, all of them seemingly sedated by a quietness that contrasts the parade we have just enjoyed.

"It has to be weird, different, foreign," Jerome emphasizes as he takes a seat at the bar. "This can't be a safe trip—I want to be daring. We are in another country. Live life!"

The bartender understands our hand signals for a drink. He recommends a liquor for us by pouring out two amber-colored shots of Herradura. I read the bottle's label as he places it back on the shelf behind him.

We toast to Jerome's short speech—to life.

The spicy tequila burns my throat.

It is fiery like the passion I feel for this beautiful place. I am enchanted already.

I cannot remember what the rest of the night was like, save for all of the dancing. Gorgeous dancing—that is how I would explain it. No one cared that Jerome and I were inebriated. In fact, that was what connected all of us on the streets at 3 AM.

The next day, I attempted to gain my bearings and become more American. I sat quietly and drank coffee, sweet and milky.

This is what it feels like to sit in a Mexican Starbucks at 8 AM—I can never sleep in when I have drunk too much the night before.

Jerome has begrudgingly joined me, and says we need to find breakfast.

It occurs to me that we have not eaten since arriving in Mexico City.

We enjoy our coffee, drinking it much faster than I would like, and leave to find some food.

Our walk isn't long until we stumble upon a food cart. I trust it—an older woman, someone's confident abuelita, is its operator. She speaks to us rapidly, as if she knows that we can't understand her, but she still needs to vent about the injustices of life. Her voice is comforting. The scent of the food is spectacular, and I find myself unconsciously salivating as she prepares our breakfast tacos.

We eat as we walk, to where we don't know. Pork and tortillas pair well. The meat is semi-sweet but packs a punch with notes of what I decide is cayenne pepper. Jarring—that is what it feels like to know that I am only a drop of water in the vast ocean that is the world.

We are lost wanderers, but excited in our aimlessness. We end up on the corner of a street, becknoned by the yells of a man selling tickets to a tour of the Xochimilco. After buying tickets, he takes us and several other tourists to a place roughly 23 minutes away.

"Xochimilco," he exclaims. We exit the old, white van and make our way through a tienda of sorts where various people are selling touristy trinkets.

Jerome and I shrug at these items. We want the genuine Mexican experience, and not shot glasses or *I Love Mexico* shirts.

The man, shorter and browner than any of us tourists, lead us to what appears to be a dark green small river filled with boats that are colored the brightest of reds, pinks, and blues. They are elaborate, and each is manually operated by a man using a seemingly 15-foot long pole. They stab the water's surface and hit the floor of the river, guiding the boats along.

It seems like back-breaking work so Jerome and I tip our 'captain' as soon as we step onto our volcano-orange boat. The wooden boat is surprisingly comfortable, and we have a band that plays and rides alongside us in their own yellow boat. The music is loud and fast, and this clashes with the slow pace of our boats. Confusion—this best describes what a person feels while floating on a murky, green river with musicians that play music in every color except that dark green.

There is plenty of food, cooked by people on boats with grills that also float alongside the boats of the tourists. I eat carne de res con arroz amarillo, beef with yellow rice.

I am full and exhausted when we are done floating along the same river that Frida Kahlo once floated on. I feel one with the sun and people of Mexico.

Jerome and I visit some tiendas back in the buzzing city and feel like real Mexicans and not silly tourists who only want to frequent English-speaking places. Our Spanish, slow and elementary, suffice.

We eat from another food cart later that night—chicken and rice. I am reminded of my childhood in Louisiana and the similarities between Mexican food and the Cajun food I ate as a child.

Walking around and seeing what the city has to offer makes me crave a repeat of the night before. In a different bar in the Zona Rosa neighborhood, (one does not look to see the names of bars as they are Spanish names that all seem gorgeous) we drink more tequila.

Our bartender, who speaks English well, tells us that she recommends something that we must taste. We tell her we are visiting from Texas, and she pours us two shots each for free.

"Trago Reposado Tequila," she says slow enough for us to relish in its name.

"It sounds fancy," I reply.

"It's all in how you say the name."

We tip her very well and thank her for the conversation.

Freeing—this is what it feels like to talk to someone who seems so different from you but shares so much in common with you. This is also how it feels to stumble and trip along the streets of a city of over 21 million that really never sleeps after drinking two large shots of tequila that a bartender says will put you soundly to sleep.

She told no lie.

On our last day in Mexico, Sunday, we walk the streets of Coyoacan, the place of coyotes. It is some sort of colonial town of the city that has become its own region. Houses and buildings of every color imaginable line the street.

We eat more street food, relishing in the authenticity of quesadillas y sopes. *Mexican food can only be eaten in Mexico*, I tell myself.

In a plaza that houses mimes and musicians, Jerome and I sit to listen to what Mexico is telling us.

In response I ask the country, "México, ¿quién soy yo?"

In a breeze, I am told that I am an amazing human being—limitless and able to experience anything that I may choose.

For John, my friend, who is vulnerable when we talk about loving black men who have left us

Grady—that amazing man that you loved/love

did not intend to not properly love you.
He did not intend to hide you as if your beauty was something to be ashamed of.
He did not intend to hurt you by staying with his wife and asking you to be a friend.
He did not intend to let you see him with another man.
He did not intend to make you so angry that you associated love with hurt.
He did not intend to argue with you and cost you years of separation.
He did not intend to scare you with a phone call that changed your life…and his.
He did not intend to have the last word.
He did not intend to die.
He did not intend to abandon you.
He did not intend to break your heart in death.

this is not how gay, black love is supposed to work especially since we no longer have to hide, and it is so fucking unfair that this is what happened to you in your life.

Justin

Dear Justin—the most challenging student I've ever encountered—

Since black men (and black people, in general) don't hear it enough, allow me to say it: I love you.
Want to know what I feel like is one of my biggest failures in my life? Yes, you guessed it. You. A tenth grader with the energy of a tornado and the personality of a rich comedian. You were hilarious! Even when I couldn't teach my lesson because your disruptions stole the show. You were funny. You just had a comedic nature about yourself. You could genuinely ask to go to the bathroom and your classmates would die of laughter. Of course, back then it wasn't humorous to me. But, in reflecting on my life at this moment, I think it is important to have wasted a few minutes of class time to laugh at the goofy things in life. Don't we deserve to smile? To laugh? To be able to joke around even when our country is seemingly in a state of race wars? We needed laughter in those moments that we should have cried for Renisha McBride and Freddie Gray.
I cried today. I did, Justin. I cried for you. I cried for myself. I cried for my brothers. I cried for my sisters. I cried for my mother and grandmother and the countless children of color they have fed and taken care of.
You won't understand what happened since you were not there to witness it from my perspective, so let me fill you in as I recall the dialogue of the consecutive fourth day of school that you had missed. Strange. Because the worst students (behavior-wise) never miss school. This is how it went:

"Mr. Jackson, Justin went to jail."
The words of your classmates seemed unreal, though I could feel the severity of what they meant as they sliced through my skin.

"For what," I asked.

Deon spoke first. Quietly—while the others listened and corrected him every now and then with something they had heard from other students gossiping about it around school. "He stole from an old white lady," he began, "and he pulled a gun out on her and then ran from the police." He, as well as the others, scrutinized my face. I know they were waiting on a reaction. They desperately needed a reaction from the only black male teacher at their school. They needed to know what I would say; I bet most of them were trying to figure out whether I would condemn Justin's actions or if I would try and lighten the mood with statements that I usually used to inspire hope. My first words were used to do neither.

"How much did he steal?", I asked. I immediately regretted asking that question first.

Charles spoke this time. "He took twenty-five dollars."

My classroom grew silent again. My lesson covering the historical context of Elie Wiesel's *Night* wouldn't happen. Not on that day. We were fighting a war ourselves. One more insidious, might I say, than World War II.

I felt anger rising in me. I was quick to hide it from my face. I had learned to do that very well. High school students were professionals at picking up on the emotions of a teacher. I wondered if they were vultures waiting to attack my weaknesses in this moment. Or any moment. I thought about my words carefully, while indulging in the silence that was so out of place in my classroom.

"How long? How long did they give him?"

No one knew. They told me that you would go to court soon. But, they told me that you were being held on a $100,000 bond. They even told me the website to go to in order to see it for myself. We looked you up and I gasped in horror, forgetting the fact that I was attempting to remain emotionally stable in front of your fellow classmates. Your name and picture were there. And under them was an amount of money that your mother would never be able to attain while working part-time at Wal-Mart.

I cried that night while drinking an entire bottle of wine. Got drunk on a damn Monday. I couldn't fight off the sadness for about a week. There were no surprise pop quizzes for three weeks in your memory. I was too sad to see the failure of any student of color. I was tired of seeing black people fail. Even simple pop quizzes on the Holocaust.

It was then that I chose to abandon the curriculum that so many teachers before me had taught. I would be the exception, but not just because of my complexion or my sexual orientation (which definitely made me stand out as a teacher in rural Arkansas). I chose to spend the rest of the year attempting to change ideals, morals, and values. In that moment. We were going to be aware of racism, sexism, homophobia, and discrimination in any form. They were going to end by the hands of a renegade (and crazy) teacher and his 119 students. All because of one. You.

I found out later that you had been tried as an adult and sentenced to 12 years in prison.

Charity

Dear Charity,

I don't remember what day it was of the week. I don't remember what kind of candy you had purchased for us at the corner store. I don't even remember if we had walked or caught a ride from one of the many men in our city that had become instantly smitten by your looks and youth. I don't recall what you were wearing or what my brothers and I were wearing. But, I remember what you said and that it was summer. I remember it was unbearably hot. I remember it was the four of us celebrating that all our birthdays were in the month of June, as always.

I was 11 and still saying ten to everyone who inquired about my age because that's what one does when your birthday was only two days prior. Estevez, the second eldest of the five of us was nine. Estevon was, unfortunately, the youngest brother (which would make his life a living hell growing up fourth and behind three teenagers) and had recently turned five. He was old enough to walk quickly enough to keep up with us.

Anyway, we were walking (so...I do remember) to the apartment of one of your friends. It was nearby to the house. The house affectionately refers to the house in which both of us grew up. Your mother was my grandmother. Momo is what everyone called her.

As my aunt, you loved us as much as you possibly could. You were so young and we were so young, yet you did not understand that we were all confused in this world. I recall that you were had recently quit high school, 3 weeks shy of graduation. A high school senior dropout. You hadn't left the house much since the miscarriage. Dropping out was the answer to your loneliness and the evasion of embarrassment and rumors from cruel 17-year-olds. Through all of that (mostly, because I didn't understand the implications of your decision at such a young age or because my mother would murder me in my sleep if I even murmured words that hinted at quitting school) I loved you more than any of my uncles and your aunts. But, you easily won for best aunt against your sister since it was only you two to choose between. My uncles and your brothers could barely stay out of jail long enough for me to even know their names. So, you easily won by a landslide against all of your five siblings.

 I remember laughing and having fun at your friend's apartment. I remember eating ice cream and my stomach hurting from all of the junk food I had consumed that day. I remember the gay man who visited the apartment while we were there. He seemed to be about your age. I assumed he was a friend to you and your friend.

 We left shortly after you'd hugged him and told him how much you missed him.

 The walk to the house was short. Momo's gumbo was awaiting our arrival. You stopped us a few feet shy from the front door.

 "Look at me…all three of y'all." We all obliged.

 Silence was not a good thing around Aunt Charity. She laughed the most. However, this was obviously not a laughing matter.

 "Don't ever," she began, "let me find out that y'all are doing that gay shit. I'll kill you."

 Her words hit me directly. She had even been looking me in the eyes as the words escaped the confinement of her mouth.

 Momo's chicken and sausage gumbo wasn't that comforting that day. And, it wasn't comforting any day after that for the rest of my life.

 I felt the radiant yellows and invigorating oranges of her spirit before she even practically ripped the door off of its hinges with excitement. The woman with an infectious spirit and big, kind demeanor and even bigger arms appeared in front of me with much more grace than her body seemed to allow.

 Momo.

 Arms that could crush me, but instead held me with the

most tender passion and love a human being could muster swallowed my frail frame. She offered that love each and every time one of her grandchildren was in arms' reach.

It was 2015 and I was 24-years-old. And, she could still make me as happy as a spoiled grandchild who was given way too many chocolate chip cookies behind his parents' backs.

I hugged her back with as much strength as a skinny freshman in college could have. Though, my strength (or any man in my family, for that matter) could never surpass the strength of the huge-armed women who shared the last names as us.

I could feel the happiness and joy that life could give me in her presence. The house couldn't compete with her aura. It was god-like. If I asked her, she would attribute it to God and her faith in him. And, I would probably mention that God was a woman. And, she would politely listen to my reasoning and even nod her head that acknowledged some slight agreement with the fact that women gave birth on this earth and that God could only create life if the *he* was actually a woman. Then, she would tell me that was an intelligent idea and she would talk about what God has done for her in her life. I would be mesmerized and impressed with how strong she was. She would cook for me and we would share laughs as we recounted memories of the good times. Momo was never aware of the horrible times in the house that she headed.

I decided not to tell her about the words that were delivered by her daughter a few years earlier.

It was better that she did not know.

Her cooking was therapeutic. Today's meal was no exception. Beef tips with brown gravy and rice. Quick and delicious.

We sat in her two rocking chairs that were in the living room behind the brown, refurbished couch that had seen more years of life than I had. We talked of Christmas and how happy she was that I had been able to come home for the Christmas break.

The heat that came from the dollar-store heater was no less grand than the heat that came from her loving heart. Momo could make all of us feel as if we were the favorites. There were no favorites because her love was a large enough blanket to cover all of us. Every single person in the family.

These were my favorite days. She was my favorite person.

The food was filling, yet my conscious was insatiable. It was my curiosity and my need to have life all figured out that would lead to my death. I was sure of it.

"How is she? Aunt Charity, I mean?" The words didn't leave my person in a confident manner.

"She's ok."

Her eyes didn't meet mine. The TV seemed more interesting, but I knew that it was pain that kept her from looking my way.

"Is she ok? Like, really ok?"

My aunt was a touchy subject. Everyone knew not to bring her up around me and vice versa.

Momo was silent. My grandmother was never silent. But, she was thinking. She wanted to say something. She just didn't want to offend me. I knew she had taken Charity's side a long time ago. The family was divided. I didn't expect that to happen when I made that phone call two years earlier.

I chose to speak again since she didn't reply. "She's in Louisiana?"

My question was met with silence. I couldn't tell if it was purposefully done. Or, if she was thinking about the past. The past hurts. I didn't want to hurt her. I let it go.

But, I assumed Charity hadn't let it go. If given the opportunity, she would most likely slit my throat and then burn my corpse in Momo's summer-charred and unhealthy front yard.

Still, the hatred would continue to thrive in her heart since she couldn't kill me a thousand times more.

I was the reason her children were taken away from her.

And, I would do it again if given the opportunity to

restart that moment.

Jason

April 25, 2015

Dear Ross,

  You were definitely a breath of fresh air. For lack of better words, you fucked my life up in all of the right ways.
  You got to know me. Or, at least, a part of myself that I would categorize as the real me. In essence, you were able to discover the juxtaposition that I am. Though, I have no idea if that process was even bearable for you. In the year that you've known me, you've been able to share drunken nights in bed with a plethora of moans and smiles that only exponentially increased as the bottles of wine fell over empty—devoid of soul, one at a time. You've been able to clumsily dance with me to the beat of music that we both hated. You've been able to laugh at the worst puns and jokes while I've hated you momentarily for how much harder you could laugh. You've been able to penetrate my hatred and misunderstanding of others with such an innocent and loving spirit. You've been able to partially understand that my anger sometimes blinds me and causes me to become alienated from the world. You've been able to realize that your existence as a white, bisexual male differs from my existence as a black, gay male. You've been able to confirm that your very existence means benefitting from privilege. You've been able to know that your development and success as an American will not mirror mine. And, you've been able to feel that sadness because you've tasted it on my lips. Many times. You've been able to sense that you will never be able to make me happy. Not permanently. You've been able to wish to be anything except a white man. You've been able to wish to be with me. You've been able to become addicted to my scent and the sound of my voice. You've been able to affirm me by showering me with compliments and kisses on my neck. You've been able to repair me in some ways.

Because of you, I don't hate white people.
Tolerating them? I'm still working on that.

Dear Ross,

Perhaps if the flight was going somewhere else or was leaving at a different time, I would've made it. I would've rushed to the gate with everything. All of my possessions. All of my baggage. All of the love that I have to offer (which is hardly any at this point). All of me. And you would have had to accept it because once I would have become a passenger; you were going to be stuck with me. Stuck. That's the word that causes my skin to crawl. I don't want to be stuck. More importantly, I don't want you to be stuck with me. Wouldn't that be a sad life?

You asked for me to come to California. At that moment. We both know I could have. But, would I?

Throughout my life, I have realized that the choices I've made and continue to make affect who I am, the individual I see when I peer into a mirror. I want to be right for a change. I want to impact him positively, for once.

I have Jerome and I love him—more than I love you. I love him more than myself. He is my escape from the lies and hurt I've caused people in my life because he is the only person I have not hurt. I'm not a good person. I'm not trustworthy. I'm not fair. I'm not just. I'm not selfless. I am me. Complex.

I chose to miss that flight because I deserve to fly with Jerome. I prefer to soar beside him. I prefer to be stuck with someone who wants to be stuck with me. I prefer to be stuck with someone who thinks that I am the most innocent person in existence. The ticket was in my hand.

I left you standing there, stupefied.
I apologize for not loving you as much as you love me.
I apologize for caring more about myself than you.
I don't regret either.
I've hurt enough people.

For the first time, I was holistically satisfied with doing the right thing.

Dear Ross,

You don't answer my texts, calls, or emails. [I think you're smart].

only children search for everything in life

Dear Kalil,

  I know that life sometimes beats the shit out of you when you've already expressed that you're the loser. You wave that fucking dumb white flag as if it truly means that you've given up. But, you do. Because that's what society told us someone who gives up should do.
  Anyway, you wave that pitiful flag and life spits on you, kicks you, punches you, assaults you, invades you, dehumanizes you, scolds you, reproves you, abuses you, uses you. The shit hurts, doesn't it? I know it. I know pain. I know how it feels to have all of your hopes and dreams be waved away by life's bullshit and its fickle hands. I know. I know what it feels like to crave to fly and have your wings be clipped with jolts of lightning. I know.
  You called me this morning at 7 AM threatening to commit suicide. Frankly, it didn't surprise me that you wanted to reach out for help. We've discussed the pitfalls we both are currently experiencing. The shortcomings, the disappointments, and heartbreaks.
  You are gay, lonely, needy, dark-skinned, beautiful, dumb, intelligent, foolish, naïve, crazy, misunderstood. I've heard it all from you and those lovely rants that portray your desire to be loved. To be acknowledged. I know. I know it hurts.
  You wanted to jump from the I-210 Israel LaFleur Bridge in our hometown. Massive, beautiful, and breathtaking. It is. Jump into the water that leads to the Gulf of Mexico.
  Your threats of self-murder inspired me to ponder what a person would actually feel and see and smell and taste and hear as they chose to end their life. Such a fucking view. They would feel a cool breeze that would smell like saltwater and the feathers of pelicans. Wafts of the crabs that inhabited Lake Charles's murky waters would hit them with an intensity that would

probably make them think the wind had a vendetta against them. They would see some of the most amazing colors depending on what time they decided to jump thousands of feet. At dawn, the vivacity of oranges, pinks, and purples caresses your spirit. At day, the exciting bright blues and whites embrace your soul. At dusk, exhilarating reds, yellows, and teals clinch what existence you have. At night, galvanizing greens, grays, and blacks engross your being. They would want to remain alive the entire 24 hours to view the splendor of what is here. What surrounds them. What is in existence. What is reality. They would hear the constant motion of cars and the wind's breath and drunk water swaying, swaying in a dance that no one can learn to master. They would taste God. They would taste God (her or him…or it—yes, it). They would taste the sex they had and maybe never had. They would taste soap in their mouths for cursing in front of their mother. They would taste the ass-whippings with extension cords and thick leather belts that helped them build character and reminded them that mama was powerful. They would taste life.

Who would want to give that up? That sweet shit? The honey of life?

They would not answer such questions. Or, if they sought to answer them, the waters would envelope them with the force of concrete.

Don't give up, Kalil. Don't give up.

Don't give up, I tell myself. Told myself.

Don't give up, the younger me told himself when faggot was a word that could cut me. Slash my vitality. Rip my vigor. Gash my liveliness. Oh, yes, it was once possible to tear me down.

You cannot give up.

untitled

I don't know what lived in that house at 4211 Worthy Drive in Lake Charles, Louisiana, but I know that it wanted us gone. Or, worse…dead. Enistazha felt it first. She would run into my room in the middle of the night and dive headfirst into my bed, waking me up and attempting to hold onto me. I was not a supportive or particularly affectionate brother and I would pry her off of me and then escort her to her own room. She would cry—beg with every fiber of her body—for me to stay with her. I never understood what she was afraid of as she would become practically speechless when I asked her to describe what had her running out of her room at two in the morning, sheet grasped in her hand.
…
Floating on the clouds in the dark, bleak sky was a bright figure. It looked down upon me. I gently screamed to Enistazha and directed her attention to it. She smiled and began crying.

It's Jesus, I said. Whatever it was, Jesus killed it for us. Those words pacified her.

Enistazha looked into my eyes and seemed to say, I hope so.

She yawned and began to relax, pulling her sheet over herself. She was enveloped by both it and the name of who she had learned was the son of God.

I was amazed at how the name of Jesus Christ could calm and soothe the troubled souls of black people.

Today, I am not sure of what I saw or experienced. I ponder this moment often.

the internet

Have you ever googled something like, *How do I get over heartbreak* or *What to do when my heart is broken* or *Is there anything I can do to repair my fucking heart* or *Who can I talk to when I feel like the kitchen knife that I usually use to cut chicken is what I need inside of myself* or *How in the fuck am I supposed to eat at the same fucking restaurants that we once went to without vomiting and crying and feeling an anger that is indescribable* or *When does it ever stop hurting because I am sick and tired of being sick and tired* or *this shit is stupid and I just want to end it all*?

guys who haven't graduated from college, yet

January 3, 2018
    The way the sun shines on your face in this moment—your tamed wild facial hair absorbs the sun's rays and I am appreciative of how the world gives you what it has to offer. The hairs are not even and together they juxtapose the softness that encompasses your face. There is your nose and its ridge that defines it. Those brown eyes—they've seen much pain and yet you push on and fight and struggle, your calloused hands weary but young. Small, gold hoops hang onto your small ears though aren't noticeable. You've had to remind me that your ears are pierced when you catch me surveying them. Your neck is not long enough, and your chin does not sharply jut out of place, your face and head seem compact even. Missing eyelashes help to paint a portrait of who you are, and I read their gaps to figure out how much you've been through.

January 28, 2018

Ok, ok.
I know this is random. But, I have to say it.
You're amazing.
And, you'll make someone so happy, Clayton.
So, fucking happy, man.
I care about you so much.
I just want you to win.
You're so much bigger and better than me, man.
Make me proud.
You deserve the best.
I love you, man.
(16 minutes later)
I know I probably killed your mood.
My bad.
I'll keep my thoughts to myself.

(5 minutes later)

You're fine.
I just wasn't expecting it. That's all.
Get your rest.

    That's it. That's all you text back. I look at the cerulean blue messages that I've sent and then the light gray messages that you've sent in response. I feel dumb. Is this what silently chasing the idea of love feels like after your capacity to love has been snatched away out of one of the nooks in your heart?

first black editor-in-chief at my school and my staff is comprised of white women

white women are not your friends.
white women cry.
white women are not your friends.
white women recognize your kindness, a hand extended to them in hopes of being amicable, and despite that kindness, cut off your desert sand-complexioned hand, your burnt umber-complexioned hand, your russet-complexioned hand, your kobicha-complexioned hand, your taupe-complexioned hand.
white women are not your friends.
white women see your smile and refuse to believe that your goodness is valuable goodness and don't invest in you as you are the dilapidated building that houses african and latino and asian and middle-eastern people that their white men would tear down and replace with a Starbucks and an expensive condominium.
white women are not your friends.
white women walk into a room with a self-worth that has been appraised in the millions since birth.
white women are not your friends.
white women laugh at you when you admit that you have never seen or tasted beef wellington.
white women are not your friends.
white women challenge your authority when each of your individual roles have been established.
white women are not your friends.
white women are annoyed easily, and don't see you as an equal even though you drink the same caramel soy latte that they drink.
white women are not your friends.
white women complain and shrink when people of color outnumber white people.
white women are not your friends.
White women see racism at the hands of their fathers, brothers, husbands, friends and sit by idly to avoid the attention that would

then threaten their social statuses.
white women are not your friends.
White women mispronounce your name, laugh, and suggest alternatives.
white women are not your friends.
White women think that including Halle Berry in a conversation has fulfilled the unsaid requirement of diversity in white-women-centric and politically-correct conversations.
white women are not your friends.
white women are made to be so important in society that even when sharing my own experience of being a black man at a private, Catholic institution, I somehow still have to write about them in order for them to truly understand the fucking travesty exacerbated by their ignorance.
white women are not your friends.

five years ago in June

Your locs—cut them off, I once said. I like a smooth head, a haircut that is masculine and fresh and sexy.
You listened to my words carefully, thoughtfully.

Yesterday in April:
Your locs—they smell like our favorite Jamaican restaurant, I say. Like the brown stew chicken that we love, I continue. Like the vivid pink and purple planted tulips that line the entrance of our apartment complex that our dogs love to sniff on morning walks, like the buttermilk pancakes with strawberries cooked in them at Harry's near Montrose that I am fond of and you tolerate on account of my pleasing to go there for brunch every single weekend, like the freshly-cut grass and an orange-brick and evanescent sunset that invites Louisiana's mosquitoes to feast on our humidity-spritzed skin, like the virgin coconut oil we rub into the coats of two dogs that are annoyed with being shampooed with oatmeal and left to sit in a bath tub filled with three inches of water that they have assumed is to drown them with, like the argan oil shampoo and conditioner that you use every two or three days instead of the dollar-store shampoo I use since I began balding so young, like the baby's lotion you rub on my head and body when I am simultaneously overwhelmed by a lack of self-confidence induced by my two bald spots and the muscle aches, like the laundry detergent that I buy since you are no longer allowed to purchase detergent or bar soap or paper towels as you prefer products of a cheaper quality, like the cheap but delicious vegan cheese and Canadian bacon pizza I order from the place down the street that unnecessarily receives your disapproving gaze whenever I decide to bring it home, like the two-percent milk that you purchase despite my demands that we live a vegan lifestyle so as to help the cows worldwide that are milked for kids who love sugar and cereal but mostly sugar for breakfast.

You listen to my words carefully, thoughtfully.

I love you, Jerome. And, there is nothing that I could ever do in life to repay you for what you have done for me in my life. You were a light when the dark closet had already become home, when I didn't know that showing your face to the sunlight was a privilege all black boys earned.

No human being amounts to you.

The first time we made love, I was nervous. Shivering.
I could feel the aura.
This.
Was.
God.

I could feel the universe within me when we became one.

hibachi means fire bowl in Japanese

    We spent $64 that day. Well, you spent $64 that day. We sat in the ornately decorated steakhouse full of Sugarland, Texas families and held each other's hands as if the threatening stares we received didn't intimidate us.
    It was my first time in a Japanese steakhouse, and you wanted to treat me. We had come from the beach in Surfside, Texas. After your best friend begrudgingly went home after the cops stopped us and gave him a speeding ticket, you wanted to do something with me—to lighten the bleak mood police officers gifted to black men. You and I pretended we had nothing to do with him in that moment, mainly because we had already warned him multiple times about doing anything crazy near a beach full of white people. It was to be expected that they'd be watching us.
    At the beach, the water was cooler than expected. Though, the sun warmed my back. I hate remembering how your warm hand held mine the entire time, and we didn't care whose children were watching us. In that moment, it was our right to love each other.
    I had argued with my boyfriend that morning in order to escape to the beach with you. He had asked to come and I had told him that I wanted to be alone—or, something like that. I don't remember much of that, but I remember everything else.
    Flames, loud and rambunctious, seared the steak we'd ordered. I can still smell it. Rice, eggs, seasoning, charred peppers, onions, garlic, soy sauce, butter.
    I remember your smile, the way you peered into my eyes, the sound of your voice when you forbid me from reaching for the bill, the way your fingers lightly touched my back and shoulders as reminders that my body was in your arms.
    I'm your man, you had said.
    I smiled.
    I got you, you had said.

I remember that was one of the last times I trusted a man.

how to become God

Stand, dressed, in a dark room.
Think about the worst part of your day.
Cry, scream, or laugh.
Or, cry, scream, and laugh.
Think about the best part of your day.
Smile.
Light a scented candle.
Undress in front of a mirror.
Stand there for several seconds.
Simply exist.
Close your eyes and take a few breaths.
Open your eyes and gaze at your reflection.
Appreciate every single atom that comprises your body.
Explore your own body with your fingers.
Turn on the warm water in the shower.
Listen to the water as you study your reflection further.
Enter the shower.
Allow the water to touch every part of your body.
Bow your head and relax your arms.
Close your eyes.
Continuously being washed by water, simply exist.
Stand there.
Lose track of time.
Stand there until you feel free, or at least liberated.
Let it go, let it all go.

Subpoena

I changed my hair;
changed my attire;
changed the way I cry;
changed the drink I order at the bar—
and it feels so great to know that you know nothing about me—
    that there are particles of my body that you were
never introduced to,
never touched,
never pillaged for pleasure,
never had the chance to smash with your hammer or insecurities.
    I sent my lawyers to your house to retrieve the part of my soul
    I had offered to you every single time we made love.
I paid good money
for them to bring pieces of me
back to me—
so imagine my disbelief
when they told me
you'd given them nothing,
that you'd said you had nothing
and told me that you'd thrown pieces of me
into the trash along with the tissues
you used to clean yourself up
after loving a man you didn't love.

anger anger anger anger anger anger anger anger anger anger anger anger anger

I have only begged twice in my life
for anything in my life:
for you to come back
and
for God to *fucking give me sunlight* at midnight.
—he grew darker and ignored my cry
when I needed it the most and wanted to die.

beholding the photo of you and I, naked and out of the shower

we have conversations
in a bathroom mirror
speckled with filth and a plethora of runaway of water droplets.
I smell you, your chin on my shoulder
and cheek warming one of my own.
this is when the hurricane came.
Harvey.
I remember the storm before we became a storm.

discovering pieces of you when I should be finding myself

      I notice how close the complexion of Cancun's sand
      is to yours and I close my eyes
      to accept a consoling by Mexican sunlight
      since no church wants me
      and I don't know what I want
      except to be free
      from the burdens of a Wednesday
      that lacks the sympathy   that black men   that most men   that all men lack
      which prompts the question
      were all men born on a Thursday
      led by fingertips—
      of the women who were in labor on those gloriously arduous Wednesdays—
      that they grasped in tiny hands
      not yet capable of pointing out what all black grandmothers know—that
          hurt people hurt people.

they called me faggot

My mother's boyfriend—all 250 pounds of him—
meant every pound of those six letters.
The words were heavy
and my hands caught the heaviness that filled them up,
didn't allow me to touch anything else except that anger,
that resentment, that agony.
it was metallic, lousy, cumbersome, dense.
I held
on to that for so long. So l o n g.
14 years later, I let it go.
just pulled my fingers away and allowed my arms to fall
by my sides.
I let it go.

The math teacher who fell in love with me- November 2018

He said to me, *Let's talk about something that makes you happy—tell me about your favorite things.*
I love running.
The feel of the wind in my face.
The music in my ears.
The way my muscles work.
The soreness I have afterward—it indicates I've worked hard.
I love cooking.
Seeing people relish in the surprise that I know how to cook.
I love banana pudding made my grandmother in Lake Charles.
I love lasagna.
I love a fresh haircut.
I love writing.
Poetry that takes six or seven readings to get.
Reading a good book with the space heater blowing on my legs.
Warm ginger ale, heated a little in the microwave.
Hearing rain hitting concrete—and the smell of that, too.
A car driving slowly over rocks and gravel.

**The science teacher I was falling in love with-
early December 2018**

First time.

I feel better since he's been inside of me.

December 8.

The science teacher I was falling in love with- mid December 2018

      Third time. In ten days, I've learned the course of his body—my fingers have felt how successfully atoms were manipulated in his creation.
      He says, we have energy together.
      He says, that's scary.

The science teacher I was falling in love with- late December 2018

    Though your body is composed of shards of glass that cut everything and everyone, they scrape against my skin like the warm water in your shower that I wished we could have felt at the same time in the beginning. I can't feel the pain, yet. Is this what six-year-olds experience before they notice that cut on their legs and plead with their mothers to help alleviate the pain that suddenly appears to collect a debt.
    Making love to you is a fascinatingly vulnerable experience—how many times did the richness and depth of your thrust translate into heroin that surged throughout me and caused my legs to quiver?
    We lie in bed afterward listening to soft music that has become laced with marijuana and fingers that probe my body.
    And, I enjoy it.
    I take a shower with you now.
    Though, you'll deny ever touching me even though you have tasted atoms of my body whose sweetness lured the warmth of your tongue and you have experienced home every single time you felt and then lived inside of me. And, despite knowing this, I still invite you inside.
    Why do I insist on being the place you call home?—where you should feel safe and free from what it means to live a life of lies because I know what you want and need. You are loved when you love me and this is why you will be embraced by the community of one
        that waits for you.
        Every. Single. Time.

The science teacher I was falling in love with- early January 2019

We get high.

I contemplate.

I've tried so diligently not to become concrete after the first time my heart was broken. I've willed myself to be cotton candy. I do not want to be adobe clay hardened by incessant sun when you are finished with me.

The science teacher I was falling in love with- mid January 2019

I think about how I'm going to die all the time, he says. I feel as though I'm going to die young, he continues. That declarative statement leaves his tongue as if it's the first time those words have been allowed to leave his front yard, as if they were newly given permission to go out into the world.

The science teacher I was falling in love with-
13 February 2019

    We smoked on the concrete patio of his uncle's house—black people *do* own houses. The notion is unreal to me even as an adult who society demands should buy a house. We lie in his bed in silence until I broke what is invisibly heavy with a usual contemplative, carving tone that could be interpreted in various ways. This was, in some instances, to my detriment.
    I ain't even said nothing and I said something, huh?
    My tone was natural. I didn't wait on an answer to this first question.
    His head swayed toward my voice, but he seemed to remain still.
    We high, I declared, aware and proud of the succinctness of the use of African-American Vernacular English. The way I allowed the word to leave my mouth resulted in a higher-pitched 'huh' type of inflection. The pronunciation. His tongue was lighter. There were molecules of ambience beneath those exits of sounds. There was an overwhelming and delightful guillotine of vowels and syllables. What was within the sounds of that aura?—Its being light yellow and beyond the edge of the universe's hiss and slither. This was a Snapish, J. K. Rowling hegemony of its legendary hiss. The buzz. There was glory. There was the movement. There was the laughter of a person. Aside from the person. No, an individual. Aside from the person. Devoid of the flaws that would make a person a person. There was color. There was vividness. There was the master. There was the artist. The creator. The artist that the author created because only an author who knew how to give birth to the skills that would be beneath him and in the created could do so.
    He talked about his mother and his father and his sisters and how they knew. He knew that they knew but alluded to a decision to not hurt his mother. How long would it hurt her, I indiscriminately inquired. I attempted to maintain an inflection of

awe and curiosity so as to not reveal my disappointment in realizing he wouldn't ever allow me to meet the individual he spoke of frequently. Forever, he replied. His tone didn't rise as his inflection mirrored his decision, written in stone. I grew tired of processing the definition of inflection.

I peered at him.

He was a sculptor, and it is why I found myself gravitating toward his energy.

I met God, I said. I met God seven times. I looked away from him as I said the words. I knew what God was to him.

Though, he seemed to not realize what God was to me.

It was the opposite for me. When he said it, I could feel an energy that was lethargic and dark. His words ushered in a ghastly mood—for several seconds, we existed in an energy that could not be described—not even by the word, indescribable.

We lay in silence for moments. I don't know for how long—time is a man-made construct.

You met the devil, I asked.

I had to face what's at my core, he said.

I didn't immediately respond with a factual, me, too—though, I desperately desired to share something in common with him.

I met God seven times, I repeated, overwhelmed with awe. I was saying the words for myself now, and not for him. My body shivered, my senses simultaneously dull and sharp.

In actuality, I had not known for sure if it was five or six or seven or even four, but seven felt right. Intrinsically, it made sense. He drew back and gasped—he was standing at this point, standing over me and looking down at me in disbelief as if he was shocked I could experience something of the sort. No! No, he said. That's blasphemous, he exclaimed. He pretended to hit me in jest, zealously and convincingly so. But, yet so serious, so steadfast in his attempt to persuade to not believe what I now believed. I told him everything that when he asked what I saw, what did I know.

Everything, I said. Everything is everything, I elaborated.

What does that mean, he asked. I could see frustration in his eyes despite the nervous, perplexed smile worn on his face.

I bent down when God stopped above me in the bathroom. I was in the universe, but I was in the bathroom.

God showed me what had to happen before you die. I felt it with my own soul. It sounded silly to write, and I should have known that it would sound sillier to him.

Perhaps, because it was his bathroom, he could not understand that the universe had existed within such a small space of five feet.

I lay in his bed beside him, looking him the eyes. I tried to explain, but he could not understand. He asked what I meant.

What I mean, I began again, is that I met God seven times. Seven fucking times.

He did not accept what I was saying. You're high, he said.

No, you're high, I responded.

He fathomed what I said. Or, at least, he attempted. This happened in between bouts of silence that exacerbated the tension that he felt and the same tension I could feel but did not accept.

I now understood.
I now understood that he would not ever understand.

The science teacher I was falling in love with-
18 February 2019

Heartbreak is lying on your back and navigating the fine hairs on your abdomen with my slender fingers and realizing that I will faintly remember what this moment felt like when you cross my mind randomly in a year and a half.

The science teacher I was falling in love with-mid-late February 2019

    We got high and he lay a cover on the half dying, half thriving yellow-green grass in his uncle's backyard. It was his idea. We lay there, hoodies and sunglasses on in 80-degree-or-so weather, experiencing the sun. In that moment, I pitied people who would never know what we felt for those two hours as our bodies radiated energy. I told him that I could feel the earth's magnetic pull, my body being tugged at by something that beckoned my core. A piano's tranquility enveloped my body and kept me grounded when my brain panicked. But, I felt him beside me and that panic became a calmness.

    I try not to remember all of the details and only the highlights. It'll make it easier to forget him when he breaks my heart.

The science teacher I was falling in love with-
mid-late February 2019

      You fucked me to songs that helped me articulate why and how I was falling in love with you. They were a background soundtrack to a conquistador penetrating a concubine.
      I realized you had played this playlist for men before me.
      I wept when you finished and turned the other way.

The science teacher I was falling out of love with-
9 March 2019 [10 March 2019 in Shanghai]

    I sat at a café in Shanghai, China, satisfied, after reading—or attempting to read—an issue of Vogue China.
    Thinking about him.
    I texted him.
        You'll read my book when it's finished?
    He replied.
        I would.
    I noticed the possibility that he wouldn't when he utilized the word *would*.
        Promise. With the words, I will.
    My message went unanswered.

    I realized that even though hundreds of thousands of people will read my writing, the man I finished this novel for will not. That is the truth that hurts so badly.

Made in the USA
Monee, IL
06 January 2020